# OATH TO A
# WITHERED
# STAR

Joseph Young

OATH TO A WITHERED STAR

First edition. November 18, 2025.

Copyright © 2025 Joseph Young.

ISBN: 979-8999907714

Written by Joseph Young.

# Table of Contents

# Dedication

To the readers and dreamers who turned the page,
and found a universe waiting,
you are the reason these stars shine.

To my wife, Sam - Your love steadies my orbit and
gives this journey meaning.

To Lucille and Lynden - You are my brightest lights,
my greatest adventure.

And to everyone I've ever called family whether by
blood, by bond, or by time, your belief in me shaped
every line, every battle, every breath of this story.

This book carries pieces of all of you.
Thank you for walking beside me through every
chapter, on and off the page.

—Joseph Young

# Chapter 1

## DAWNFALL DESCENT

**T**he descent into Velmora felt like dropping into a furnace wrapped in static. The stormfront ahead was thick with ion haze, and the clouds below shimmered faintly.

**Captain Aris Solene** stood at the helm of the Zephira Dawn, boots braced, one hand gripping the rail beside her. The ship trembled beneath her as it resisted gravity's pull. Ahead, the atmospheric sheath of the planet rippled in unstable layers, some electric, some dense with particulate ash.

Aris was strikingly beautiful in ways that seemed unpretentious. Her dark hair was tied back in a short twist, a few strands loose from the static in the air. She wore her armor without flourish, and still it fit her like command. Aris looked every bit the captain, but there was something quieter beneath the surface, a tired warmth in her eyes, the kind that suggested she hadn't always lived on edge. Years ago, she'd worn a uniform in Olyssian colors, serving in the very fleet that now hunted her. Leaving hadn't been survival. It had been defiance.

Once, she might have been someone who laughed easily. Now, she was someone who was holding herself together through sheer strength and determination. But at the helm, with the stars before her, she could still remember the joy.

In moments like these, flying the Zephira Dawn felt like holding the reins of the cosmos itself. The controls yielded to her touch as if they knew her mind, each adjustment sending the ship gliding with effortless grace. The low vibration of the drives thrummed through the deck into her bones and the faint scent of ozone and warm circuitry hung in the air. Beyond the viewport, the stars unfurled in endless silence, and the curve of the planet rose to meet her, bathed in shifting light. Here, she could enjoy the unbroken freedom of the sky, and the quiet joy of knowing it was hers to command.

Her mission intelligence of the planet's inhabitants hinted at potential trouble. Her history with the Olyssians might only make things worse.

"We're holding altitude," said Ralik from the nav station. "But we're hitting interference. Magnetic spikes every twelve seconds."

**Ralik Aeran** was smaller in build, thoughtful and precise, with a soft voice that often got lost under engine noise. He wore a hybrid headset that wrapped from his jawline to his temple, constantly syncing with the ship's data feed. The interface lights reflected off his skin in shifting patterns as he adjusted the stabilizers. His posture was always tight, like he expected things to go wrong. He'd grown up on Talrin Station, where preparing for disaster wasn't pessimism, it was survival. Mostly due to his home world staying neutral while the rest of the galaxy tore itself apart.

From behind him a rougher voice cut in. "Why can't we ever have a smooth landing?"

**Thorne Kaid** stood at the weapons console, not yet strapped in. His frame was broad, his shoulders too wide for the harness he half-ignored. Scars trailed along his forearms like old brushstrokes, uneven and unhidden, and somehow blended seamlessly with the full-sleeve tattoos that wrapped around them. It was hard to tell where ink ended, and history began. He had a fighter's build, a criminal's posture, and the kind of face that dared someone to ask what he'd done to get here. He rarely talked about his years before joining the crew, but they knew his past wasn't perfect. He'd once served in the Olyssian military, drafted out of Carrion Reach, a hard-edged colony world known for breeding soldiers with more grit than mercy. Despite his gruffness, there was something protective in the way he lingered near the crew during turbulence, just close enough to react if something went wrong.

"You could try not jinxing us," Ralik muttered without looking up.

Thorne grunted and finally dropped into his seat. "If we crash, I want it on record that I called it."

"If we crash, there won't be a record," Ralik replied.

"Both of you lock in," Aris said.

The comms chimed with a sharp tone. Ralik's visor lit with movement. "We've got contact," Ralik said. "Multiple ships. They're repositioning into a tight blockade around the descent corridor."

The forward display adjusted, lighting up with six vessels in a layered formation just above Velmora's upper atmosphere. The Olyssian ships were sleek, black-plated, and wedge-shaped with no external markings. They were military, no question. Each one was twice the size of the *Zephira Dawn* and positioned like a trap already sprung.

"They're sending a docking request," Ralik reported. "Strict protocol format. No weapons, no orbital engagement."

"Doesn't mean they won't bring both," Thorne muttered.

"They're boarding soon," Aris said quietly. "Ralik, drop shields and prep the airlock. Keep the Dawn powered. If things go sideways, I want to be able to launch right away."

Ralik gave a stiff nod. "Understood."

The Olyssian vessel latched to the Zephira Dawn with a low groan of magnetic clamps. Seconds later, the outer hatch cycled, and the airlock hissed open.

Four soldiers entered through the airlock in matte black, visors down, rifles held vertically. They stepped in with the precision of people trained not to hesitate. Behind them came their commanding officer.

She was tall, lean, and severe. Silver accents lined her high-collared uniform, and the black of her coat seemed darker than her escort's armor. Her hair was cropped close on the sides and swept back above sharp, unreadable eyes. Her features were familiar in a way Aris couldn't quite place. Her face had sharp angles, similar bone structure, enough to catch her off guard for a moment.

Her aura was deliberate. Controlled. Like a storm, tightly sealed behind polished boots.

"I am Commander Tavarin. Authority over Velmora's southern hemisphere under Executive Accord Order 7-19-Delta. Your presence in this region is a violation of Olyssian planetary restriction zones."

Aris kept her arms at her sides. Not at attention, not relaxed. "We're operating under a civilian contract with an independent ecological council."

Tavarin scanned the ship interior without moving her head. "Your ecological council doesn't exist in our records."

"It does in mine," Aris replied.

Tavarin took a step closer, the guards holding formation behind her.

"There are extraction protocols in place for this planet," she said. "Mining surveys. Active containment zones. Your arrival complicates a closed operation."

Aris didn't blink. "We're not here to interfere with Accord logistics. Our terms are limited to survey scans and environmental stability reports. Our time on the surface will be brief."

Tavarin's gaze sharpened. "Convenient story...One you've used before, I suspect."

"You've reviewed the clearance," Aris replied. "Yet you boarded anyway."

"I prefer direct clarification," Tavarin said.

"Then clarify something for me," Aris said. "Are you denying our landing outright, or just letting us wonder if you'll shoot first next time?"

Tavarin studied her. She didn't blink often, but a corner of her mouth ticked upward.

"You're here for more than flora," Tavarin said calmly. "I could lock this down with a single directive. And yet, here we are."

Aris tilted her head slightly. "And you're here for more than enforcement."

A pause stretched between them. Tavarin's expression didn't change, but her eyes narrowed the slightest fraction. Whether in suspicion or amusement, Aris couldn't tell.

"I can authorize a limited corridor," Tavarin said at last. "Forty-eight hours. Five-kilometer radius. You don't scan outside your zone. You don't deploy anything airborne. And if you stray from that agreement, the Accord won't issue a second warning."

Aris gave a small nod. "That's acceptable."

"Good," Tavarin said, turning back toward the airlock. Her guards moved with her, fluid and practiced.

She paused at the threshold, back still to Aris. "One more thing," Tavarin said. "If I find out you're operating under false directives, I'll personally escort you off this planet. That version of our conversation will not be as civil."

Aris didn't flinch. Her tone stayed level. "I wouldn't want to waste your time twice."

Tavarin said nothing further. The hatch sealed behind her with a final hiss.

Thorne let out a quiet breath. "That felt like a conversation between two knives."

The contract had been for ecological scans. Nothing more. But Aris hadn't taken this job for the money, and she hadn't come to Velmora just to study the trees. Whatever the Olyssians were doing here, it was bleeding into places it didn't belong.

"She gave us a corridor," Aris said, already turning back to the cockpit.

"She also gave us a timer," Ralik added, tapping his display. "They've carved a narrow descent lane into the lower shelf. If we drift off it, their sentries will light us up."

"Then we don't waste time," Aris said. "Ralik, prepare for landing."

"Engines steady. We are ready to enter Velmora's atmosphere." Ralik replied.

Aris tapped her comm. "Fen, you ready?"

Down in the forward hold, **Fen Orlan** stood beside the cargo lockers, checking over his gear with quiet precision. He was broad-shouldered, clean-cut, with a steady presence that seemed to settle the air around him. His armor was minimal, reinforced only where it mattered, and scuffed from use. There were faint markings beneath the scuffs, symbols from his home colony on Lutharia, a place he rarely spoke of and never planned to see again.

He didn't speak immediately. He always measured his words before spending them. He joined the crew to provide security, especially where Olyssians were concerned.

"Everything's in check," Fen replied, tightening a chest strap. "We're good on our end."

Across from him, perched casually on a sealed container, **Pixo** watched with slow blinks and rhythmic sways of his tail. Small and feline in posture, he was covered in smooth, silken fur. Though he bore the features of a cat with large ears, narrow frame, and sharp eyes, he stood upright, walking on two legs with an easy, almost mischievous balance that was uniquely his own. Pixo was from Monalaria, a temperate moon known for labyrinthine forests and cities built in the trees. His kind rarely left their home planet, believing that the outside worlds were cursed.

Pixo tilted his head. "You always check everything twice."

"Only when we land somewhere new," Fen said.

Pixo gave a toothless smile. "I'd trust your gear more if the dirt wasn't staring back."

Fen gave him a sidelong glance. "You're not helping."

"I wasn't trying to," Pixo replied, tail flicking once before he hopped off the crate.

Fen exhaled through his nose, then sealed his helmet without another word.

The *Zephira Dawn* sliced through Velmora's cloudline with a muffled groan, its hull sheathed in refracted violet light. Below, the planet revealed itself slowly, like light creeping over the horizon. Sprawling jungle blanketed the surface in deep, layered greens, but laced through it were strange, unnatural hues:

bioluminescent purples traced the treetops like veins, while thick canopies glistened with wet, translucent petals in impossible shades of lavender and plum. Everything shimmered slightly, as if the air itself were steeped in unseen energy.

"Visual confirmation of landing zone," Ralik reported from the co-pilot seat, his voice calm despite the anomaly in their descent scans. " Atmospheric energy fields are fluctuating with irregular magnetic patterns. Something is interfering with the sensors. It's not natural weather."

Aris leaned forward, narrowing her eyes as the ship broke through a final wall of mist. The jungle below didn't just look alive...it felt aware. The planet's surface pulsed, not with machine signals or radiation, but with something more primal. She adjusted their course as the landing struts deployed with a metallic hiss.

The *Dawn* settled on a moss-covered shelf tucked between towering foliage. Soft steam bled from the vents as the engines wound down. Outside, vines coiled lazily over stone and tree alike, and strange spores drifted through the humid air in slow, deliberate spirals. The area was entirely silent, with no wind or sounds; everything remained still throughout the jungle.

"Let's not assume quiet means safe," Aris said, already heading toward the ramp. "We'll need clean readings before we move deeper. Pixo, Ralik, get the station gear prepped. Fen, Thorne, you're on security perimeter sweep."

Thorne cracked his neck as he finished checking the power cells in his gauntlets. "Got it."

Fen nodded silently, adjusting the straps of his chest plate. The ramp lowered, revealing a world swathed in color and mist. Every tree trunk looked older than it should've, growth rings too thick, bark patterns stretched in ways that spoke of centuries, not decades. The bark webbed with bioluminescent moss. Ferns the size of sailcloth swayed without wind. The ground was soft, layered in fibrous growth that resisted slightly under each step.

Thorne and Fen moved first, their boots sinking quietly into the spongy terrain. Each movement stirred loose spores, which danced lazily before settling again. They advanced in practiced formation, eyes sweeping the foliage, weapons at low-ready but fingers tense.

Then something shifted. Between two broad trees, just beyond a thick curtain of violet vines, something moved. Yellow eyes blinked once from the shadows. The creature crouched low...tiger-like in form, but too fluid, too silent. Its skin rippled between bark-like armor and fur, cloaking it in perfect camouflage.

Then Fen's voice crackled into comms, cautious. "I'm picking up some kind of animal in the trees."

Aris straightened. "Clarify."

"I can't get a clear visual, it's camouflaged. It's...large."

There was a pause.

Thorne's voice came low. "It's just watching us..."

Then it turned and vanished into the forest, silent as breath. None of them moved.

"Log it," Aris said quietly. "And pull back."

She didn't ask questions. Not yet. Whatever was out there hadn't bolted in fear. It had withdrawn. Deliberate. A predator's patience. And that was worse.

# Chapter 2

## VELMORA S VEIL

Captain Aris Solene waited at the base of the ramp, her twin pistols holstered, one hand resting on the rail. Beyond her, the jungle pressed close, thick with violet mist. Fen and Thorne emerged from the treeline in formation, boots leaving faint impressions in the spongy ground as they crossed back to the ship.

"Report," Aris said, her gaze tracking their movements.

"Perimeter's clear," Fen said, unclipping his helmet. "Aside from the...thing."

"It saw us," Thorne added. "But it chose not to engage."

Aris nodded once. "Copy. We weren't expecting hostile alien lifeforms. Let's all stay sharp."

Inside the *Zephira Dawn*, the soft hum of systems diagnostics filled the silence beneath the tension.

Thorne sat near the hatch, adjusting the emitters in his power gauntlets. The plates hissed faintly as he recalibrated the shield cores, three slim status lights along his wrist blinking green. The tech wasn't fancy, but in his hands, it became a shield when it mattered most. Thorne didn't talk much about what he did before the crew. He didn't have to. The way he stood between danger and the others said enough.

Fen rechecked his rifle at the weapons bench, not because it needed it, but because it helped him think. He was quiet in a unique way. With calm hands, and a steady gaze that anchored the group during their recovery. They were supposed to be here for a scan and survey, not creeping through alien forests with their weapons half-raised. He thought about the potential dangers they could encounter on the planet.

Ralik hovered beside the systems console, brow furrowed over a customized sensor relay. His device flickered with static, struggling to process readings from the canopy above. "I can't get a clean map. Still too much electromagnetic distortion from the upper atmosphere."

"Can it be filtered?" Aris asked.

"Not unless we stay still for three hours. And we're not doing that." He said.

"You're right. This planet's beginning to seem hostile. We must keep moving." She moved toward the rear of the ship where the outer ramp met the jungle's edge. A thin layer of pollen shimmered in the air like dust

caught in sunlight. The trees didn't sway, but
something about them felt...attuned.

Aris paused, gaze lingering on the twisting vines that
draped from branches like veins.

Thorne came up beside her. "I don't like how quiet it
is."

"You never like how quiet it is," Ralik said, descending
behind him, his sensor rig already humming with
distorted readings. "Though for what it's worth, you're
not wrong."

Aris didn't respond right away. She adjusted her belt,
checked her pistols, and started down the ramp
without a word.

Pixo followed, cradling a half-assembled device in one
hand and a coil of wire in the other. "So, this is
Velmora," he said, eyes not on the jungle but on the
mess of parts in his grip. "Can't wait to see what I can
make out of this place."

The team moved in a loose wedge formation, boots
sinking into moss that pulsed faintly with
bioluminescent rootlight. It was soft, like veins under
the skin. Above them, the canopy filtered daylight into

bands of gold and green, but nothing chirped. Nothing called. It was as if the world had dimmed its sound in anticipation.

Aris led with twin pistols holstered at her hips, her strides purposeful. She spoke only when necessary, but the way her head tilted with each shift in wind betrayed her alertness. Their route angled northeast, toward the center of the jungle flagged for elevated radiation, one of several key sites marked for ecological scans.

Thorne brought up the rear, gauntlets charged to ready status, each movement deliberate. His presence was a wall behind them. They passed a fallen branch as wide as a speeder. Its bark had been stripped away, green tendrils threading through the break like muscle beneath skin, still faintly pulsing.

Pixo slowed, glanced around. "Anyone else feel that?"

Thorne didn't stop walking. "Feel what?"

"I felt a small tremor," Pixo stated.

"I felt it too," Fen said quietly. "Like pressure under the ground."

Aris raised a hand to halt them. "Everyone keep your eyes peeled for movement."

Ralik tapped the side of his visor, activating a translucent scan overlay. Data shimmered across his lens. "I'm picking up massive energy spikes across the foliage."

A vine overhead twitched.

"Hold," Aris said, pistols already sliding into her hands with practiced ease.

Another vine slithered slowly along a tree limb above, its texture barklike but moving far too deliberately. Then it dropped quickly as it headed straight for Pixo.

Thorne moved faster. He threw his arm forward, and the gauntlet on his wrist flashed to life, projecting a curved energy shield between Pixo and the vine. The impact rang out in a dull clang, the barrier glowing yellow from the force.

"Hostiles incoming!" Thorne barked.

More vines stirred, unfurling from branches and roots, moving like animals with muscle and intent. Several lashed forward from the underbrush, striking fast and coordinated.

Aris opened fire, crisp energy bursts slicing through two vines mid-snap. They recoiled with a shriek, their ends writhing as if in pain.

"Ralik, find their host!" she ordered.

"Too many spikes to triangulate," he said, sweeping his visor to manual targeting. "They're all around us."

"Backtrack to the ridge hollow!" Aris commanded.

Fen flanked Thorne, rifle raised. "Go, I've got you covered!"

As the vines lashed closer, Pixo crouched, tail flicking once before he sprang, landing neatly on Fen's back. "Hope you don't mind," he muttered, gripping a strap on Fen's shoulder harness. "Better view from up here and fewer things trying to eat me."

Fen didn't flinch. "Long as you don't start narrating again."

"No promises," Pixo grinned, fumbling through his satchel with quick, practiced paws. He pulled out a thin injector, its casing marked in bright yellow.

Fen flinched as Pixo jabbed it into his shoulder. "Stim boost. Try not to bite your tongue."

Fen's eyes widened as the effects kicked in. His grip tightened on his rifle, and he surged forward with renewed speed.

"I could get used to that," Fen muttered.

"Let's hope you don't need another," Pixo replied, already scanning their surroundings from his perch.

All around them, the jungle had turned predatory. Vines struck like whips, some sprouting thorned tips mid-lash. The air was thick with spores and the bitter scent of decaying flora.

Thorne barreled ahead, deflecting attacks with his energy gauntlet, which flashed from yellow to orange and back again. "This isn't just flora. It's coordinated."

Ralik's visor cleared with a flicker as the interference dropped, the readings finally stabilizing. He snapped his baton out, cracking it across an attacking tendril before ducking behind a root cluster. "Confirmed! All tendrils are linked to a sole source, up on that ridge!"

Aris was already moving, twin pistols firing with surgical precision. Each blast severed a vine but more took its place. "Cover me!"

She charged ahead, carving a path toward the rise. The team followed, shields flaring, sensors buzzing, branches and roots lashing from the undergrowth in a frenzy.

And then they saw it. Towering over the clearing was a four-meter-tall monstrosity composed of fused vines, bark, and gnarled root plating. The core pulsed with violet light. From its 'shoulders' sprouted massive tendrils tipped with jagged hooks, and its mouth opened like a wide bloom that was thorn-lined, and breathing hot, noxious air.

The ground shook with its steps.

"We're not retreating. We have a mission to finish." Aris yelled. "Split and circle it!"

Fen peeled left, Thorne right, drawing the monster's attention with wild swings of his shielded arm. One tendril crashed down. Thorne met it with his shield as sparks flared, and he was thrown back several feet, crashing into the mud.

"Still alive!" he called, coughing.

Aris rolled beneath another flailing limb and fired directly into the beast's side. It scorched the bark, but it was barely fazed. "The hide's too thick!"

Ralik's visor flared. "Target the exposed node at the base of its back side!"

"I'll get it!" Fen yelled, skidding behind a fallen branch. Pixo, still clutching his back, tapped his shoulder urgently.

"Left knee vine, it's prepping to lash!"

Fen ducked just as a tendril sliced the air inches above them.

"I love you, little guy," Fen muttered, charging forward again.

Thorne took another hit, and his shield gauntlets flashed red, then failed completely. He dropped to one knee, gasping. "I have no more shield charges!" he barked.

"Fall back!" Aris called.

"Negative. I won't leave you!" Thorne gritted his teeth, leaping up to land a punch with his gauntlets on the beast's side. A hooked tendril snapped around his arm, dragging him toward the creature's thorn-lined maw. Its jaws clamped down, scraping across his gauntlet as he wrenched free. It turned, snarling, and that gave Fen an opening.

Fen dove beneath the beast's body, sliding in the muck, and jammed a plasma charge into the exposed root-knot on its spine. "Charge set!" he shouted, scrambling out.

"Fire in the roots!" Pixo squeaked from his back.

The explosion was absorbed by flesh and bark but effective. The beast shrieked, spinning wildly, tendrils flailing in every direction.

Aris seized the opportunity. She sprinted up its shoulder, pistols glowing white-hot, and unloaded both barrels directly into its upper node.

The beast's shriek pierced the clearing. It twisted, spasmed, and finally collapsed, toppling in slow motion as its limbs dug trenches through the earth. Steam hissed from the remains, and violet sap bled from the wounds.

Thorne staggered to his feet, armor scraped and shield smoking. "Please tell me that was the last of them."

Aris didn't answer. She stood panting atop the corpse, staring into the jungle ahead, as if already bracing for the next. They hadn't planned to pick fights with the wildlife. They were here to finish the scans, to complete the mission they'd already risked too much for.

Ralik used his visor to log scans of the dead fauna. The results indicated a positive ID of their mission objective. The planet seemed connected in a way that was unexplainable. They couldn't leave until they finished the job. Failure meant more than wasted time, it meant no pay, no ship, no second chances.

Later, just beyond the scarred clearing. The Zephira Dawn's crew gathered around a slowly forming camp: a half-ring of thermal lights embedded into the earth, casting a pale warmth onto the foliage. The downed creature's body was far enough behind them that the scent didn't overpower the air, but close enough to remind them how easily the mission could have ended there.

Thorne sat near the perimeter, slouched against a trunk with a stim patch on his shoulder and a cracked gauntlet laid beside him like a sleeping animal. "I'll be feeling every hit in the morning," he muttered.

Aris knelt by the portable heater, feeding in a power cell. "You did well back there."

Thorne scoffed lightly, shifting his weight with a wince. "Yeah? Feels like I got hit by a shuttle."

Aris didn't smile, but there was a softness behind her eyes. "Still standing."

"Barely."

Across the camp, Fen crouched beside the firelight, running a cloth over his scratched sidearm. The warmth danced across his features, making him look younger and less like someone who had just fought for his life.

"You helped provide the opening," he said without looking up. "That counts."

Thorne raised an eyebrow. "Pretty sure it just got bored of chewing on me."

Fen glanced over, a flicker of a grin tugging at the corner of his mouth. "Then you make a lousy appetizer."

"Appreciate the image," Thorne laughed.

Behind them, Pixo was curled near Fen's pack again, legs crossed, tail flicking occasionally as he adjusted a small gadget with careful claws. He hadn't said much since the fight, just the occasional click of tools or low hum of concentration. It was quite typical for a Monalarian to busy themselves with building something, especially when stressed.

He looked up now, ears twitching. "Just so we're all clear, I'm not designed for combat stress. You nearly lost your best gearsmith to spontaneous cardiac arrest."

"You mean you almost panicked," Thorne said.

"I did panic," Pixo corrected with a huff. "But constructively." He went to work fixing everyone's gear and weaponry.

Ralik, visor lying beside him, finally broke his silence. He had that deep-focus expression again, eyes trailing something only he could see.

"The root network, it wasn't random," he said quietly. "It responded the moment we stepped in. Like it knew where we'd be."

Thorne raised a brow. "Plants with telepathy now?"

Ralik shook his head. "Not psychic. Just...connected. I think everything here might be part of a system. One we haven't even scratched the surface of."

Aris leaned back against a fallen log, eyes on the treeline where that monstrous vine-thing had come from. Nothing moved now, but still, she didn't relax.

"We hold here tonight," she said. "No heroics. If something moves, you wake the others."

Fen nodded. " I got first watch."

No one argued.

They all knew the truth: whatever had happened today was only the beginning. Velmora had noticed them. Now it was watching

# Chapter 3

## TWILIGHT S TEETH

ris stood on a shoreline that bent reality. The stars above her weren't distant points of light but hung impossibly close, low enough to touch, their glow distorted and slow like fireflies caught in tar. The sea that met the dark horizon wasn't water as she knew it, but something heavier, thicker, a tide made from memory and weight. It lapped at her boots in complete silence, not a single wave breaking, not a single gull in the sky. Only her breath echoed in her ears. It was shallow, restrained, as if even dreaming she didn't dare take up too much space.

A figure waited in the surf ahead, just far enough that she couldn't see his eyes but close enough that her heart recognized him before her mind did.

**Samir**. He stood like he always had before a combat drop with his spine half-cocked, shoulders too relaxed, and that damned crooked smile that said *this'll be easy* even when it never was. The Olyssian fatigues were wrinkled like always, the sleeves shoved up past his elbows. His hand was outstretched, palm open, fingers loose.

He was waiting for her to come closer. He always had been.

Her legs moved before she realized it, her body drawn forward like a thread pulled through cloth, but the second she crossed the waterline between them, the sea surged. Not toward her, but *through* him.

It ripped him apart, not violently, but deliberately, like paper unraveling under a slow tear. The tide swept away what was left. Not blood. Not ash. Just the space he used to occupy.

She screamed without sound.

And then she was standing alone again, waves brushing her ankles, stars flickering above as if they were trying not to look at her.

Aris woke hard, her lungs dragging in air like she'd surfaced from deep below.

The camp was dim, washed in the soft flicker of thermal lights. She stayed still for a moment, her eyes tracing the outline of the clearing, half-expecting to see the ocean still swelling around her. But all that met her was moss and shadow and the ache in her chest.

She sat up slowly, dragging her jacket around her shoulders with mechanical familiarity. The dream still clung to her like damp fabric, and no amount of rational thought could shake its weight. She hadn't seen Samir's face in a long time. She didn't know why now. *Was it because of Velmora?* She wondered. Maybe it wasn't Velmora itself. Maybe it was just easier to blame the planet than admit she was already on edge. Planets like this had a way of digging up things you thought you'd buried.

Aris put her elbows on her knees, her hands began rubbing her forehead, as if she could scrub the dream from her brain. The jungle's breath was still all around her. She didn't realize Ralik was watching until his voice broke through the hush.

"You all right?"

She didn't look at him at first. "Just a dream."

He shifted slightly but kept his eyes on the ground between them. "Didn't sound like just a dream."

Aris huffed out a breath, part laugh, part defeat. "Are you always this observant?"

"It comes with the job." He gave a small shrug. "Reading things no one says out loud."

Normally, she wouldn't have answered. Normally, she'd have let the silence close the door. But something about the jungle, the fight, the exhaustion...or maybe just Ralik's quiet way of waiting, made it easier to let the words out this time.

There was a long pause. She picked at a loose thread in her sleeve. "I dreamed of someone I knew. A long time ago."

Ralik stayed quiet, but it was the kind of silence that made space rather than filled it.

"His name was Samir. We served together." She hesitated. "He...died on a mission I sent him on."

Ralik finally looked up, his voice low and his eyes softened. "And you blame yourself?"

"I was the one who told him to go back," she said, barely audible. "I was so stubborn in following orders, I lost track of the dangers involved."

"Do you miss him?" Ralik asked gently.

"Every day. Even on the ones where I try not to." She let her hands drop. "He was reckless. Too charming for his own good. He always made everything seem easy, even when it wasn't."

Ralik was quiet again but not gone. "I'm sorry."

She looked at him then, really looked. "Why do you even care?"

"I don't know," he admitted. "But I do." It was honest. A little awkward. But honest.

Aris gave a small nod, her expression somewhere between pain and gratitude. "Thanks."

Ralik looked away again, tugging at the frayed strap on his sleeve. "I'm not good with this kind of thing. Just so you know."

"You're doing fine," she said, voice soft.

He cleared his throat once, like he wasn't sure if he was going to speak again but did anyway. "I had a brother once," he said, voice quiet.

Aris turned her head slightly. She didn't interrupt.

"Not by blood. We grew up in the same orphanage sector. Shared everything. Rations, hiding spots, even a bunk once." He gave a faint, almost bitter laugh. "We used to say the universe owed us something."

"What happened?" she asked gently.

Ralik shrugged, a motion that looked heavier than it should have. "He joined the Olyssian naval program when we turned sixteen. I didn't."

"Why not?" Aris asked.

"It wasn't my dream." He paused. "But I knew I couldn't stop him from chasing after his."

Aris followed each word closely, tracing the intent behind them and the spaces where meaning lingered.

Ralik looked up at the stars for a moment before his gaze dropped again. "I always wonder if he is still out there among the stars."

Aris watched him for a moment, her expression unreadable in the half-light. The fire cast a soft shimmer across the clearing, flickering shadows over the sharp lines of her face.

"I hope he is," she said finally. "Even if you're not with him, it doesn't mean he's not with you."

Ralik nodded slowly, jaw tightening just enough to show that the words landed somewhere deep. "Yeah. Maybe that's enough."

Aris drew in a breath and let it out, quieter than before. "Sometimes I think forgetting might be the kinder thing."

Ralik glanced sideways at her. "Are you talking about your dream?"

She didn't answer right away. Her thumb traced a slow circle against her palm, as if the movement might stir the right words loose.

"It felt like he was right there," she said quietly. "Close enough to touch. Like if I just reached a little further..." She let the thought trail off, shaking her head. "Then it was all gone. No warning. Just emptiness. Like I made him up just to miss him."

Ralik was quiet for a beat, then said softly, "I'm glad you're the one leading us."

Aris glanced over, surprised by the simplicity of it.

He didn't elaborate, he didn't need to. The words hung in the space between them, honest and steady.

She gave a small nod, barely more than a breath. "Thanks."

The fire cracked softly, the low hum of the ship's systems pulsing behind them. Velmora's sky above wove thick clouds through faint, scattered stars, the whole expanse caught in a restless struggle over what to conceal.

Then the comm unit on Ralik's wrist let out a sharp ping, drawing both of their attention. He tapped the display. "Inbound distress signal. Olyssian encryption."

Aris rose to her feet, all softness gone from her posture. "Can you trace it?"

Ralik was already pulling his visor back over his eyes. "Working on it. It's a faint signal." A few seconds passed in silence but for the quiet clicks of his interface. "I've got a location. Just past the ridge, three klicks southwest."

Aris didn't hesitate. She shouted to everyone at camp. "We've got a distress signal from an Olyssian source. I know this isn't the intended mission, but I will not ignore someone in trouble. Moving out in five."

Around them, the crew stirred. Fen was already lacing his boots, eyes sharp even through the haze of sleep. Thorne groaned from his spot against the trunk but reached for his restored gauntlets without complaint. Pixo, bleary-eyed and halfway tangled in a thermal blanket, muttered something about ill-timed emergencies but began packing his gear.

Five minutes later, the team moved through the dark, low-lit jungle in staggered formation. Ralik led, visor glowing a soft blue as he tracked the signal through distortions. The forest grew denser the farther they walked. Vines looped low like nooses. Bark shimmered with bioluminescence in deep reds and purples. And through it all, that unsettling quiet.

"Signal's steadier now," Ralik murmured. "We're close."

They broke through the final tree line to a clearing of broken metal and charred earth. An Olyssian tech outpost, or what was left of it. Half the structure had collapsed, steel twisted into spiraled ruin. The other half leaned at an unnatural angle, its antenna array snapped like brittle bones.

"Damn!" Fen breathed. "What did this?"

Thorne crouched near a drag mark etched deep into the dirt. "Something strong. Real strong."

They moved in cautiously. Inside, the damage was worse. Claw marks raked across walls and consoles, long and uneven, as if the attacker hadn't just tried to kill, but to dismantle. Two bodies lay near a collapsed console, charred and partially buried under debris. Federation engineers, judging by the scorched insignias. Ralik knelt beside one and tapped his visor, activating a light scan.

"No signs of pulse. These guys didn't die from the collapse, their wounds were internal."

"Any data we can pull?" Aris asked.

Ralik moved to the central terminal, the last piece of equipment still sputtering light. He tapped a few commands. "Encrypted, but the drive is intact. Give me a second."

The screen flickered, stabilizing just long enough to flash several garbled lines of code. Ralik squinted, running a diagnostic override. Bits of text began sliding down the screen, but they were broken and incomplete.

*LOG ENTRY 240-C*

*PROJECT: HEARTSPIRE*

*Structural readings unstable...root interference increasing beyond safe parameter.*

*Team Theta reassigned to outer perimeter after...exposure incident.*

*Central node shows rhythmic pulses that are believed to be reactive, possibly aware.*

*Lead tech Smith requesting reinforcement from orbit or immediate shutdown authorization.*

*Command response delayed. Signal degraded. Holding position until further...containment breach likely...is not dormant.*

The cursor blinked at the end. Nothing else followed. No one spoke at first. Even the jungle outside held its breath.

Thorne exhaled through his nose. "Well. That's not unsettling at all."

Aris stared at the screen, jaw tight. "They knew something was wrong."

"More than wrong," Ralik murmured. "They were left without reinforcements."

Pixo shifted nervously atop a storage crate, his tail twitching behind him. "I'm sorry, but did we just casually scroll past the phrase containment breach like that's not a full-on panic flag?"

Fen leaned against the doorway, arms folded. "If there was a breach...where's the breach now?"

A tense silence followed.

Then Aris, steady and quiet: "Gone. Or still here." She turned toward the others. "If we leave now, we walk away blind. Whatever this project was, it ties to the readings we've been tracking. If we don't figure out what Heartspire is, someone else will, and they won't be half as careful. Either way, we're not leaving without answers."

Thorne let out a dry chuckle. "We never do."

A metallic glint caught Aris's eye beneath the wreckage of a shattered terminal. She crouched, pushing aside a loose panel. Nestled in the cracked remains of a containment cradle was a small vial. It was cylindrical, capped in silver, and pulsing faintly with an eerie, purple glow.

"Careful," Ralik warned from behind her. "That's not just decoration."

Aris held it up to the light. Inside, wisps of energy curled like smoke with nowhere to go.

Pixo crept closer, eyes wide as the vial's glow pulsed against his fur. "That's root energy. Refined. I've never seen it in liquid form."

He sounded more curious than alarmed, but even Aris knew how rare it was to see root energy harvested this way. Valuable in the right hands, dangerous in the wrong ones, but not why they were here. Their mission was still focused on answers, not resources.

Aris studied the vial for a beat longer. "Well, now you have." She handed it over, her tone calm but tight. "Treat it like it bites."

Pixo took it gingerly, tucking it into a padded pouch in his satchel. "I'll try not to shake it."

"Don't," Thorne said, glancing over. "If that thing goes off in your bag, I'm not hauling your toasted tail back to the ship."

Pixo gave a dramatic sniff. "Noted, Sergeant Sunshine."

Ralik knelt beside the fractured machine where they'd found the vial, fingers brushing over the blackened housing. "Whatever they were doing here...it wasn't just mining." His visor pinged faintly as he swept it over the interior. "I'm getting faint energy dispersal patterns heading east. Same type as the vial."

Aris straightened. "Could be residual trail from the breach. Let's follow it."

They moved with purpose now. The forest had a way of swallowing sound, every step muffled under moss and hanging roots. The faint glow of disturbed foliage led them deeper, where the air grew cooler and heavy with damp rot.

Fen held his rifle low as they approached a narrow ridge. "There are marks nearby," he muttered.

At the base of the incline, deep gouges split the earth with claw marks. Four-pronged, wide as a man's chest.

Ralik crouched. "This could be the breach. Pressure on the outer edges...this thing was wounded."

A distant snarl echoed through the trees.

They didn't speak again until they reached a broad clearing ringed in jagged stone. A cave entrance loomed ahead, half-choked by roots. Fen zoomed in with his rifle scope as he noticed a prone human crawling backward towards the entrance, one leg dragging behind him.

"Olyssian uniform," Aris said, her voice tense.

The wounded soldier cried out, trying to raise his sidearm with a shaking hand.

Then the trees in front of him exploded. A monstrous creature bigger than anything they'd seen before appeared, its frame filled the clearing in a blur of muscle, moss, and root-wrapped fur. This creature was unlike anything in their registry. One eye glowed faintly with a sickly red hue, the other was scarred shut. It lunged forward, jaws split wide in a roar that rattled the stones.

"Move!" Aris shouted.

They split. Fen dove left, drawing the beast's gaze, while Thorne sprinted into the clearing and yanked the Olyssian soldier clear with one arm. A swipe from the beast's claws tore a gouge through the rock where the man had just been.

"Circle it!" Ralik called, visor flashing symbols across his display. "It's slower on the left side!"

Aris fired her pistols in tandem, each blast slamming into the beast's flank, but it barely flinched.

Behind her, Pixo froze, eyes wide as the creature roared again. The vial in his satchel glowed through the fabric, pulsing in rhythm with the monster's snarls.

The wounded Olyssian, half-conscious, caught sight of it and shouted hoarsely, "The vial! You must drink it!"

Pixo blinked. "Me?!"

"Just do it!" The soldier yelled as the creature bore down on them again.

Trembling, Pixo yanked the vial free. "This is definitely not medically approved," he muttered as he popped the seal.

The liquid shimmered like starlight. He hesitated one heartbeat too long. Then he drank.

His body convulsed once, twice...then expanded, limbs stretching, muscles thickening with unnatural force. His back arched, spine crackling with energy. A glow spread beneath his fur like lightning caught in water.

Fen gawked. "Oh stars..."

Pixo hit the ground with a thud that cracked a stone slab beneath him. He looked up. And growled.

The forest shuddered as Pixo straightened to his full height, now easily matching the beast in size. His normally lean, wiry frame had shifted into something primal and powerful, but his eyes were still his own, wide with disbelief, yet glowing with adrenaline.

The creature snarled, confused by the sudden shift in its prey's posture. It hesitated just long enough. Pixo didn't.

With a roar that was far deeper than his voice had ever been, he launched himself forward. The two titans collided in a crash that shook the treetops. Claws met claws, fur met bark. The impact sent a wave of cracked roots and splintered stone outward like shrapnel.

Thorne dove over the Olyssian soldier, shielding him with a half-powered gauntlet just before the shockwave hit. "Okay. That's new."

"Pixo just body-checked a monster," Fen said, ducking beside him. "Go Pixo!"

Pixo grappled with the beast, massive paws gripping the creature's forelimbs as it thrashed. The vine-fused beast wrapped one tendril around his torso and slammed him into a boulder. The rock cracked, but Pixo surged back to his feet, tail lashing through the air like a whip.

Aris fired again, the blasts drawing the creature's attention just enough for Pixo to land a crushing punch to its ribs, followed by a thunderous shoulder tackle that drove the beast back toward the cave mouth.

Ralik's visor pulsed with overlapping energy signatures, data streaming too fast to process in real time. "The root resonance is burning out," he called out, urgency creeping into his voice. "Pixo's not going to last much longer in that form."

Aris didn't hesitate. "Then we end this now. Give him a clear path with coordinated fire!"

The crew moved as one, instinct overriding fatigue. Fen broke left, circling through the underbrush with his sidearm raised. He fired in short, controlled bursts, herding the beast's attention away from Pixo. Thorne moved in tandem on the opposite flank, his gauntlet humming with strain as it deployed a crackling barrier just in time to deflect a thick vine that whipped dangerously close to Ralik's chest.

"Appreciate it," Ralik muttered, already adjusting his targeting overlay.

Aris darted forward, rolling under a low swipe of the creature's clawed limb. Coming up from the spin, she fired both pistols in tandem, bright arcs of plasma carving scorched lines across the beast's shoulder and jaw. The shots staggered it for half a second...just long enough.

Pixo, towering and panting with the effort of holding his transformed form together, launched forward like a boulder unchained. He slammed into the beast with his full weight, claws locking around its torso in a primal grapple. The creature roared, roots flailing and lashing wildly around them. Dirt exploded as the two massive forms fought, crashing against stone and uprooting the forest floor in a quake of limbs and muscle.

"You've got this, buddy," Fen muttered from behind cover, eyes scanning for any opening to assist.

Pixo let out a strained roar as he warped through the last of the root's energy surging through him. Muscles trembling, he drove his claws deep into the beast's flank. The creature howled in agony, its massive form buckling as glowing violet ichor burst from the wound in a shimmering arc. The fluid splattered across the twisted ground, sizzling against stone and moss alike.

The beast reeled, limbs flailing in violent spasms, but it didn't fall.

"Now!" Aris shouted.

Thorne didn't need the cue twice. He charged forward, one gauntlet raised, the other already surging with overclocked plasma. As he neared, he slammed both fists into the open wound left by Pixo. There was a rising hum, then a burst of white-hot light as his shield deployed from the inside out.

The force sliced through the beast's core with surgical precision. A pulse of energy rippled outward as the creature arched in its final death spasm and then split apart, cleaved cleanly in two by the expanding energy.

The two halves of the beast collapsed to the earth with a thunderous crash, steam and violet mist rising from the ruptured body like a dying breath.

Pixo staggered back, rapidly shrinking, the glow around him fading to flickers. He dropped to one knee, exhausted and trembling, the empty vial still clinking faintly in his satchel.

Thorne stood beside the wreckage, smoke trailing from his cracked gauntlets. "That," he muttered, catching his breath, "was too damn close."

Aris knelt beside Pixo, steadying him. "Pixo, I am impressed!"

He gave a groggy blink, eyes still wide from the surge. "I feel like I bench-pressed a moon," he mumbled, tail twitching weakly. "And then got crushed by it."

Thorne limped over. He gave Pixo a light tap on the shoulder, careful but respectful. "Didn't think you had that in you."

"I didn't either," Pixo replied, managing the ghost of a grin. Then a weak groan reminded them they weren't alone.

"Help me with him," Aris said, already moving toward the injured Olyssian soldier they had pulled to safety just before the beast charged.

Fen and Thorne gently lifted the wounded man, cradling him with care as they brought him toward the edge of the cavern, away from the stink and still-spasming limbs of the slain creature. They laid him against a cool slab of stone, near the filtered glow of Ralik's makeshift light beacon. His uniform was torn, soaked in blood, and his breathing came in uneven pulls, but he was still conscious. Aris crouched beside him and attempted to wrap bandages around his wounds.

"You're safe now," she said, voice low. Ralik knelt nearby, visor already scanning vitals, but the shake of his head told Aris what she didn't want to hear.

The Olyssian soldier gave a hollow chuckle, breath rasping through clenched teeth. "Safe," he echoed, his voice thin and ragged. "That's a word I haven't heard in weeks."

His gaze drifted to the cavern ceiling, unfocused, as Aris tightened the bandage around his ribs. Blood still seeped through.

"Our mission was going smoothly when we first arrived here months ago," he continued, voice low and cracked. "The root energy when we first tapped it...it was stable. Golden-blue. Pure. We harvested it, refined it, built weapons you wouldn't believe. Personal shields, rifles that bent gravity, armor that made you move like light. Our battalions were unstoppable."

Fen shifted, listening intently.

"Then...we got new orders. 'Accelerate extraction. Shift to Phase Two. Project Heartspire.' That's what they called it."

Aris exchanged a look with Ralik, who silently nodded. The soldier coughed, blood dripping from the corner of his mouth. "That's when things changed. The energy...it came out wrong."

"Wrong how?" Thorne asked, crouched beside him now.

The man blinked slowly. "The color changed. It turned purple. Dark. Almost alive. We thought it was a denser variant. The scientists were thrilled...said we'd unlocked a deeper layer of the root. They even called it a breakthrough."

His eyes fluttered. "Then the tremors started, and these mutations started emerging from everywhere."

Aris leaned in. "What caused them?"

"I don't know. Something shifted in the lower mining shafts. We lost contact with two teams. The rest of us pulled back. But then that thing found us."

He exhaled slowly, and it lingered like the last word in a long, unspoken sentence.

"We weren't ready for that," he murmured, and then he was still.

The quiet crept in like mist. Thorne adjusted the soldier's arm across his chest.

Pixo's voice broke the silence. "He really thought they were making progress."

The quiet stretched. Aris stood slowly, brushing dirt from her hands, eyes lingering on the body. "He wasn't lying," she said softly. "They really *did* think they were building something better. But they didn't understand what they were waking up."

"No one ever thinks they're digging their own grave," Thorne muttered.

Ralik stood as well, visor dimming. "The Olyssians may flag us for delay. If we don't report back to our ship and Command, we won't have time to explain a detour...let alone a trail of corpses and two dead mutations."

Aris didn't answer right away. "That soldier wasn't a rebel," she said quietly. "He followed orders. Dug where he was told. Used the tech they gave him. And it still killed him."

Thorne crossed his arms. "You think that's our fight now?"

Aris looked at her crew. "Each of us has been burned by the Olyssians in our own way. They took something from all of us: family, futures, freedom. They don't change. They just bury the wreckage and start over."

She looked toward the ruined outpost, her jaw tightening. "This Heartspire is just another cycle of their rot. Another mistake they'll try to hide until it kills more people. I won't turn away from that."

"We weren't sent here to play watchdog," Ralik replied, voice even. "We're a civilian analysis team on a clean survey route. But considering how our command's already on thin ice with the Olyssians, this changes everything. If we deviate from our original mission, we risk setting off a war."

Aris nodded once. "Exactly. And yet, here we are. A trail of dead soldiers, fractured root veins, and a creature that doesn't even exist in the registry."

Pixo shifted uncomfortably. "So, what...we just keep digging into Heartspire and hope they don't catch on?"

Aris weighed her words. "We came here to map Velmora because command needed intel on Olyssian infrastructure. Environmental data, root energy activity, any signs of weapons development. Our job was to keep it clean and quiet by finding survey routes, resource zones, transport lines. Officially, it's about risk assessment. Unofficially...we were here to see what the Olyssians didn't want anyone seeing."

Fen frowned. "What about Commander Tavarin's orders?"

"Commander Tavarin is not my commander." Aris said defiantly. "And I'm done taking orders from the Olyssians.

Thorne finally spoke, voice low. "This isn't like you, Captain."

Aris turned back toward the cave entrance. "It wasn't. But I've seen their corruption firsthand. I know how this ends if we turn our backs on it. Not this time."

A beat passed before she stepped forward, deeper into the cave. "We will log what we find and report back to command when we leave this planet."

"And if command asks for an update, before then?" Ralik asked.

Aris didn't stop walking. "Then we'll have already found something worth the risk."

Joseph Young

The others exchanged uncertain glances, but one by one, they followed. Whatever the Olyssians were hiding...it started here. And Aris had just chosen to follow it.

# Chapter 4

## ORDERS AND OUTLAWS

The crew entered the cave and soon, the tunnel opened wider than expected. It was cut cleanly, reinforced with old Olyssian alloy plating, and braced by root-wrapped pylons humming faintly with residual charge. The further in they moved, the more artificial the space felt, as though the planet had been split open and stitched back together with steel.

Aris led the way, her silhouette sharp in the dim glow of Ralik's visor beacon. She kept one hand near her sidearm, the other on her scanner, though the device had long since given up trying to label what they were walking into. The further they descended, the more the walls pulsed with dull light, a residual energy from the planet's root system, veined and flickering like an exhausted heartbeat.

"Picking up motion ahead," Ralik murmured, scanning. "Grid pattern movement. Miners, possibly support crews. Thirty, maybe forty signatures."

"Mining operation?" Fen asked, adjusting his pack.

"More than that," Ralik replied. "Looks like a full-scale extraction unit. Industrial-grade. Some of this gear's not even standard issue anymore."

Pixo looked up at the ceiling, noting the lines of industrial lighting pulsing across root-covered beams. "Nice to know the death tunnels come with lighting this time."

Thorne grunted as they reached the edge of the tunnel, eyeing a pair of guards in matte-black armor stationed across the way near a rail platform. "Don't get too cozy. We don't want to alert the Olyssians that we are here."

The cave opened into a vast chamber that was staggeringly wide, which dug deep into Velmora's bones. Dozens of steel platforms hung in tiers like a suspended city, each one crawling with workers, engineers, and reinforced machinery. Massive drills screamed against the stone, driving into clusters of luminous roots. Transport skiffs drifted between support beams, ferrying crates of harvested material toward a central refinery tower where flames flickered unnaturally blue.

The roots themselves pulsed faintly with light, a murky violet, like something tainted by heat and pressure. The deeper the veins ran, the more jagged and twisted they appeared, almost like they were resisting the machines clawing them apart.

"Stars," Fen whispered. "This is a massive mining operation. It seems more than standard resource mining."

"I agree," Aris said, eyes narrowed. "This should be part of their project Heartspire."

Her gaze locked on the far side of the cavern where a massive alloy door dominated the background. It was half-covered in scaffolding, bearing a faded insignia of the Olyssian Accords.

Aris stared a second longer, then turned from the overlook. "Let's move," she said. "No need to linger."

They descended the grated walkway, following a path that dipped beneath the main platform level. Here, the clang of metal was less constant, the heat less choking. The scale of the operation began to feel more personal. Workers passed them by in clumps, their faces smudged with dust and fatigue, suits unzipped, shoulders slack. Nobody questioned the crew's presence. No one had the energy to care.

The corridor narrowed and bent sharply left. That's when they heard music. Low and lazy, a tinny rhythm drifting out of a half-sunken bulkhead repurposed into a doorway. An old ventilation grate had been torn away, replaced by a dangling tarp marked with graffiti and chalk. A rusted metal sign leaned crooked against the wall, its painted letters faded but legible enough:

**THE TAPROOT**

Pixo stopped short, one brow raised. "Well, at least the Olyssians are consistent. Wherever they dig, they drink."

"Hard to blame them," Fen said. "I'd want a few drinks, too, working this deep."

Ralik scanned the door briefly. "Minimal movement. About twenty people inside, mixed groups. Heat signatures static and relaxed."

Aris stepped forward. "We blend in. Listen. Stay sharp."

Thorne frowned. "We really doing this?"

She gave him a look. "If there's talk happening anywhere down here, it's over drinks."

He didn't argue. They slipped through the tarp and into **The Taproot**.

The bar wasn't large, but it was lived-in and carved directly into the rock, its walls uneven and patched with scraps of plating and cloth. Light came from hanging strips of recycled glowpanels and a few flickering lanterns hung from steel rods. The air was heavy with smoke, sweat, and something sharp that might've been distilled root extract.

A dozen tables were scattered around the room, composed of old mining crates and scrap-fused benches. Off-shift workers lounged in slouched postures, talking over the static-punctuated music leaking from a speaker in the back. No one looked up when they entered.

The crew settled near the far corner, at a table beneath a broken vent that occasionally hissed lukewarm air across the room. Aris took the seat with a view of the entrance. Habit. Thorne sat across from her, arms crossed, always watching. Fen and Ralik scanned the space with quieter eyes, while Pixo leaned back, already eyeing the taps behind the bar.

A miner with oil-stained hands and a synthetic sleeve was laughing loudly in the corner, recounting a story involving a root drill and a crate of stolen food rations. Another group of engineers passed around a deck of bent cards, placing makeshift wagers in data chips.

Despite everything they'd seen above, the Taproot felt normal.

Pixo returned from the bar a few minutes later with a tray of unmarked cups. He set them down and took a cautious sip from his own, wincing.

"I think this qualifies as a chemical weapon."

"No one asked you to drink it," Thorne said.

"I'm committed to the mission," Pixo replied solemnly, setting the cup down like it might explode.

The crew shared the briefest moment of quiet. Of camaraderie. A reminder of what *normal* used to feel like. But beneath it, there was a quiet thread of unease, a tension in the laughter, a hollowness in the smiles. The kind of silence people only carried when they knew something was wrong and they weren't allowed to say it.

Aris let her eyes drift to the entryway again, her instincts prickling. Her instincts didn't need a reason. Not yet. But she felt something was coming.

Pixo had just finished his second grim sip when Aris shifted, eyes flicking toward the booth one table over. Two miners sat hunched close, shoulders nearly touching, speaking just above the music. One of them was a grizzled man with gray streaks in his beard and a patch covering one eye. He slid a tarnished flask across the table.

"Command says we're close," he muttered. "Deeper than they expected, but the readings match. Same pulses, same density shift."

The second miner, younger, with oil-stained gloves and a nervous twitch in his jaw, leaned in. "They think it's real, then?"

The older man shrugged. "They wouldn't be spending this much fuel and manpower for nothing. They want the Heartspire. And we're almost on top of it."

The rest of the sentence was drowned out by a round of laughter from another corner, but it was their first clue of what Heartspire was.

Aris's gaze narrowed slightly. Across from her, Ralik was already typing something into his wrist module under the table, logging the phrase silently.

Fen met Aris's eyes. He didn't need to say anything. They had confirmation. Whatever the Olyssians were doing down here, it wasn't aimless. The Heartspire was here, and they were digging toward it like it was salvation or a weapon.

Before Aris could signal the others to move, the air shifted. The **entrance hissed open**. The conversation dropped.

**Commander Tavarin** stepped inside, flanked by two armored enforcers in obsidian plating. Her eyes moved slowly through the haze of light and smoke, unhurried, but locked in like a targeting system. And then they landed on the crew. Aris didn't move. Tavarin didn't blink, but she smiled.

"Well," she said, "what a pleasant surprise."

Aris didn't answer. She rose slowly, pushing her chair back with deliberate calm, eyes never leaving Tavarin.

Around them, the hum of conversation faded into a brittle silence. A few workers slipped quietly away from nearby tables. Others stayed, watching with curiosity. This wasn't their first time seeing something go sideways in the Taproot.

Tavarin strode closer, posture sharp and sure. Her Olyssian coat was spotless despite the grime of the cave, and her voice carried that familiar mix of control and disdain. "I told you to stick to the civilian route. And here you are, sipping with the locals like you belong."

"I didn't know this sector was under blockade," Aris replied evenly.

"It's not," Tavarin said, stopping just short of their table. "But it's also not part of your assigned corridor. That makes this a violation. And I'm tired of pretending you don't know exactly what you're doing."

Thorne shifted slightly in his chair, tension building in his frame. His fingers hovered inches above the activation studs on his gauntlets.

Pixo leaned forward, murmuring under his breath, "Please tell me someone here has a better escape plan than *flip a table and hope for the best.*"

"No need to escort you off the planet," Tavarin added coolly. "Just a cell. All of you."

Ralik spoke quietly. "Two enforcers. Rear hallway."

Aris gave a single, subtle nod. She knew what came next. Then Tavarin's lieutenant reached for his belt. Aris moved first.

The table flipped, drinks and metal clattering to the floor. Fen fired from the hip, his pulse bolt slamming into the wall beside one of the guards. Screams filled the room as the Taproot exploded into motion.

Workers dove for cover. Bottles shattered. A beam of light sliced the haze above their heads.

"Back room!" Aris shouted, covering the team as Fen scrambled across the floor, dragging Pixo toward the rear exit.

"It's sealed!" Pixo yelled, slamming into the bulkhead. "No release panel, someone locked it from the outside!"

Ralik cracked his baton across a guard's legs, dropping him, then slipped behind an overturned bench. "Perimeter grid's active. They cut us off before they even walked in."

Thorne growled, "We're boxed in."

Aris weighed it. Two exits blocked. Six soldiers incoming. Civilians screaming in the background. Her team was exposed but not broken.

She stood. "Cease fire!" she shouted, lifting her hands above her head.

Thorne turned, stunned. "Captain..."

"I said stand down!" Aris barked, stepping clear of cover. She looked directly at Tavarin. "You want me. Fine. I'll go. But you let them walk."

Tavarin straightened, eyes unreadable beneath the blue gleam of her visor. "You don't get to dictate terms."

"You shoot through us, you'll leave plenty of your guards' bodies behind and my crew will make you wish you hadn't. I surrender. Alone. They walk.."

A long beat passed. Then Tavarin slowly lowered her weapon. "Drop your gear."

Aris unfastened her harness and sidearms, letting them fall with a soft clatter. Two enforcers approached and clipped cold magnetic cuffs to her wrists.

"Take her to central processing," Tavarin ordered. "She'll be judged under Article Nine."

As they led Aris away through the haze of smoke and upturned tables, she gave one last glance back at her crew...silent, stunned, and held in place by the weight of what had just happened. She didn't say a word. But the look in her eyes was clear: **This isn't the end. Get ready.**

# Chapter 5

## BEASTS AND BONDS

The Taproot had emptied fast. After the last shot was fired and Commander Tavarin's enforcers marched Aris out in cuffs, the regulars vanished like smoke. Tables lay overturned, cards scattered mid-hand. The heat from broken lanterns still lingered, but the room felt cold as if it had been stripped of all its color.

Fen crouched near the wall, reassembling his disarmed rifle in silence. The damage to his knuckles said more than his face ever would.

"She didn't hesitate," Fen said, still pacing near the door. "Didn't even flinch when they dragged her out."

"She knew what was coming," Ralik replied. He stood with his arms folded, the glow of his visor dimmed to near-black. "Probably knew the second Tavarin walked through the door."

"We owe her," Pixo added quietly. He sat slouched against a cracked support beam, one hand wrapped around a half-drunk metal flask. "Not just for the bar. For everything. She's been shielding us from the worst since our first mission together."

"We can't repay that by sitting here feeling sorry," Thorne said, standing. His voice wasn't angry. It was just focused now. "If we wait, she could die. We need to move."

"Move where?" Fen asked. "We don't even know where they are taking her."

"We have to try to find her," Ralik said. "Article Nine is almost certain death."

Everyone stopped.

Ralik nodded toward the scorched floor where Aris's gear had been dropped. "Tavarin mentioned it just before they walked her out."

"That's a trial sentence," Thorne said darkly. "No jury. No defense. Just survival. It's how they get rid of prisoners without calling it an execution."

"I heard some of them make it out," Pixo muttered. "But none of them stay whole."

Silence fell again, heavier than before. Then a voice spoke from the far end of the room. "You've still got a chance. If you're willing to take it."

They turned, half-expecting another officer but instead found a lone miner stepping cautiously between the debris. He was older, beard streaked with soot and silver. He wore a maintenance vest two sizes too big. A permanent limp marked his right leg. His eyes were sharp. And he wasn't drunk.

Thorne narrowed his gaze. "How can we trust you?"

The miner held up his hands, palms open. "You can't...but I'm here because I've seen what Article Nine looks like. And I don't believe she deserves it."

Ralik tilted his head. "But you work for the Olyssians?"

"I've worked logistics down here since the first root vein cracked open," the man said. "I've seen crews vanish behind that gate, one after another. It's not a trial. It's just theater. One-sided. No one's meant to walk out."

He reached into his vest and pulled out a worn keycard, its edges scuffed, the Olyssian logo barely visible through the grime.

"This'll get you through the personnel access tunnel on the backside of the gate complex. It's used by maintenance and cleanup teams. Not on the public grid."

Fen hesitated. "Why would you help us?"

The miner's expression shifted, tired but firm. "Because I've worked for the Olyssians for a long time. They aren't the shiny federation that everyone sees on the news. They are corrupt. Evil. It's time that I make amends for helping them."

He held out the keycard. Pixo took it carefully, staring at it like it might vanish.

"She doesn't have long," the miner said. "You want her back? You'd better move." Then, without waiting for thanks, he turned and disappeared out of the bar, fading like he'd never been there.

Thorne strapped his rifle to his back. "No more delays," he said.

Ralik nodded. "We find her."

Fen turned toward the broken exit, jaw tight. "And we bring her back."

Pixo slipped the keycard into his coat, a small grin tugging at the edge of his mouth. "Let's go crash a show."

Below the refinery tiers and behind the blast-sealed corridors of the lower complex, Aris found herself alone.

The walk here had been quiet. No commands, no guards barking orders, no ceremony. Just the steady sound of her boots echoing against reinforced flooring and the soft hum of security systems cycling behind the walls. Her cuffs had been removed without a word at the gate. Not as a courtesy, just a formality. They didn't need restraints now. The arena was its own prison.

The room she stepped into was round and cavernous, carved directly from Velmora's lower strata. It wasn't a cell. It wasn't even a courtroom. The walls were marked with deep carvings that were part machine-cut, part worn by time and ritual. Torchlight lined the edges, casting uneven shadows across the cracked stone. The air was warm and thick, carrying a faint stench of rust and root rot, the kind that clung to your lungs whether you wanted it or not.

Above her, a gallery of glass-paned observation decks overlooked the space. Figures watched from behind the reinforced barriers. Faceless, expressionless, and stripped of accountability. She couldn't see their eyes, but she could feel them. Their presence wasn't curious or concerned, it was clinical. They weren't here for justice. They were here for spectacle.

At the far end of the chamber sat a cage. It was enormous, its bars bent outward at the base as if something had tried to escape rather than be let out. The metal was scorched in places and stained in others. Several heavy chains snaked from the top corners to bolt anchors buried in the floor. Inside the cage, something moved...slowly, rhythmically. A scraping sound echoed faintly through the chamber, claws dragging against stone in a pattern that felt too steady to be mindless.

A voice crackled through a recessed speaker, cold and devoid of inflection. "Subject Captain Aris Solene. Trial protocol commencing under Article Nine."

Aris looked up but didn't respond. There was nothing to say. No one to appeal to. This wasn't about arguments or records. This was the part where her fate became theater.

The cage's locking mechanisms groaned and hissed, then released with a heavy metallic slam. For a few long seconds, nothing emerged. Then the shadows shifted and something massive crawled forward into the torchlight.

The creature that stepped out of the cage moved on thick, knuckled limbs, its hulking frame hunched forward beneath the weight of its own mass. Its torso was layered with **reinforced bone plating**, like a natural exoskeleton grown over muscle and root. Thick cords of bark-wrapped sinew bound its joints, flexing with each deliberate movement. Its arms were massive, longer than its legs and ended in wide, blunt claws that scraped and cracked the stone beneath it as it moved. Root-like tendrils coiled across its back and spine, glowing faintly with that same violet hue Aris had seen in the walls, as if the creature had *grown from the planet itself.*

In one of its gnarled hands, it dragged a **massive club**, crudely fashioned from a broken tree trunk fused with twisted metal and fossilized root. The weapon was twice as tall as Aris, stained dark along its edges from past use. It wasn't just a tool, it was part of the creature, an extension of the violence it had been bred or built to deliver.

Its eyes or what passed for them, burned with dim, steady light. They weren't wild. They were focused. Intent. As if whatever intelligence lurked inside that thick skull wasn't primitive...but practiced.

The moment the beast charged, Aris sidestepped on instinct. Its club smashed into the stone where she had just been, the force rippling through the ground and sending a spray of dust and debris outward like shrapnel. She tumbled across the arena floor, boots slipping on the polished blood grooves, and barely rolled to her feet before the creature thundered toward her again.

She ducked under its outstretched arm and drove her elbow into its ribcage, bone met flesh with a dull crack, but it was like hitting the side of a warship. The creature barely flinched. It swung the club again, wide and low. Aris leapt backward, but not fast enough as wood and root caught her across the thigh, and pain shot down her leg like lightning. She hit the ground hard, teeth clenched, trying not to scream.

The crowd behind the glass above remained silent. Observing. Measuring.

Blood ran down her leg. Her balance was gone. The beast stalked toward her again, slowly now, like it knew the rhythm had shifted. She backed up on all fours, gasping, trying to find an angle, a plan, anything at all. Her fingers brushed broken gravel and the smear of someone else's blood. No weapon. No escape. No backup.

The creature raised its club high. Its violet-rooted muscles surged, veins glowing. Aris could only lift her arms in a final, hopeless brace...until a sudden **flash of blue light** lit the air between her and the beast. A shimmering **plasma shield** snapped into place with a sharp *chuuum*, just as the club slammed down. The shield buckled and flared, but it held, barely.

Aris blinked, disoriented by the light, until she heard a voice grunt behind her.

"Now's not a great time to die, Captain." **Thorne** stood at her side, gauntlet planted against the shield emitter, legs straining with effort. "This creature's quite strong," he muttered through clenched teeth.

"Hold on big guy," came **Fen's voice** as he skidded to a stop behind them, rifle already snapping into firing position. The rest of the crew poured in through the **maintenance access**, eyes burning with urgency.

Ralik tossed her sidearm across the distance, and she caught it with a sharp twist of her wrist, ignoring the pain lancing through her side.

"Thought you could use these," Ralik said, coming closer and holding out the second pistol, his visor flickering with active scans. "Its armor's thicker than it looks. Aim for the root clusters along its back."

Pixo crouched beside her, quickly patching a stim injector into her shoulder. "Just enough to keep you upright. You're gonna owe me a week of ration bars."

Aris took a breath...gritted, ragged, but full. The beast roared again, shield-scorched and enraged. She stood beside her crew now, pistols primed, blood still trickling down her thigh. "Let's show this thing what we're made of."

Thorne dropped the shield. And together, they charged.

The beast was already moving before the shield flickered, its club arcing sideways in a sweep that could flatten a bunker wall. Aris dove low, sliding beneath the swing as Fen launched a shock pulse from his rifle, the blast cracking against the beast's upper shoulder. It staggered slightly but didn't fall, twisting toward him with a snarl.

"Didn't like that," Fen muttered, ducking behind a pillar of fractured root.

Pixo scrambled along the perimeter, fingers moving fast over his portable kit. "I can spike its nerve clusters," he called. "Give me five seconds!"

"Buy him time!" Aris shouted. The beast lunged, this time toward Ralik, who stood calmly as his visor pulsed brightly. At the last second, he rolled aside, dropping a **displacement beacon** that flared with a short burst of distortion. The creature's foot slammed down where he had just been, but it lost momentum, its balance faltering.

Thorne was already moving, gauntlets glowing hot. He threw his entire weight into a double-fisted slam against the beast's back leg, and bone cracked audibly.

The creature bellowed in pain and fury, spinning around but Aris was there, pistols raised.

She fired in a cross pattern, each shot aimed at the root clusters Ralik had mentioned. Her plasma rounds hit with precision, striking the exposed clusters of glowing root tissue threaded through the beast's back. The shots didn't kill it, but they burned. And they made it bleed.

The beast reared up, clutching its club in both hands, ready to bring it down in a devastating overhead slam, until a burst of static flared behind it.

"Heads up, ugly!" **Pixo's voice rang out**.

A detonation spike launched from his rig and embedded into the base of the creature's spine. The resulting shockwave wasn't large, but it was perfectly placed. The beast spasmed, dropping to one knee, its club hitting the floor with a deafening clang.

"Now!" Aris barked.

She sprinted forward, sliding between its limbs as Thorne yanked her up by the arm. She planted one foot on the club, vaulted up the creature's shoulder with her uninjured leg, and unloaded both pistols point-blank into the back of its neck. Root matter and bone exploded outward in a burst of dark light.

The beast gave one final, broken roar...then collapsed forward with a seismic thud that shook the entire chamber. Silence followed. Not from lack of noise but from awe.

Aris dropped to one knee beside the carcass, breath sharp in her throat, smoke rising from her pistols. Her crew gathered around her. She was bloodied, bruised, but alive.

Above them, the watching silhouettes behind the glass-paneled gallery didn't move. But the lights in the upper chamber dimmed. The show was over. For now.

Aris glanced up, eyes sharp and unyielding. "They wanted a trial?" she said, voice hoarse. "We just gave them a verdict."

# Chapter 6

## MUTATION AND MALICE

The maintenance shaft groaned above them as the access panel slid shut, muffling the distant echoes of the trial pit. Musty, stagnant air filled the corridor. There were no drills, no guards, just the creaking tension of silence that hadn't been broken in cycles.

Aris limped slightly, her side still bruised from the earlier fight. Thorne hovered nearby, watching for any sign she'd collapse again. She waved him off.

"I'm fine," she muttered. "We keep moving. If this tunnel leads where I think it does, we're not done yet."

Ahead, the passage sloped downward into a deeper sector of the mining system. The walls here weren't reinforced alloy anymore...they were raw rootstone, pulsing faintly with violet veins. Faint wiring was pinned across the surfaces, half-ripped out or short-circuited. Whatever this place used to be, it had long since been abandoned...or buried.

Ralik's visor pinged faint readings. "Energy spikes. Not natural. Controlled frequency, low yield. We're nearing an old lab zone."

"Military or medical?" Pixo asked, adjusting his gear.

"Probably both," Ralik said grimly. They passed through a broken bulkhead, the air cooler now, tinged with copper and antiseptic. The corridor opened into a chamber with thick observation glass, most of it cracked or smeared.

The first thing Fen noticed was the smell of stale air thick with damp stone and something metallic that clung to the back of his throat. Inside, cells lined the far wall. Dozens of them. Some were empty. Some were not.

Behind one glass panel, a figure sat motionless, face shadowed, muscles knotted unnaturally beneath sallow skin. Another cell revealed a man curled in the corner, muttering nonsense, rocking against the wall.

Then came a trail of blood, dried and dark, painting the floor and ceiling in broken patterns.

"Stars," Fen whispered, backing up slightly. "What is this place?"

Ralik crouched beside a console, fingers working fast. "This was a testing station. Logs are old, Olyssian high-security protocols. Most of it's corrupted, but I'm pulling fragments."

A few seconds passed before fragments of audio crackled to life, distorted and faint:

> *"Test subjects, batch seventeen, show increased durability...but remain emotionally unstable."*

> *"Adjusting dosage ratio of root concentrate to plasma vector. Trial sixteen underway."*

> *"Acceptable failure rate has been approved. All nonresponsive subjects redirected to holding."*

The transmission cut off with a dull static hum.

Pixo gave a low whistle and nudged a half-melted medkit with the tip of his boot. "Well, that's comforting. Good to know the Olyssian definition of 'acceptable' includes throwing rabid soldiers in jars and hoping for the best." He glanced at one of the cells, where a half-conscious subject twitched against the restraints. "Really makes you wonder what 'unacceptable' looked like."

Thorne muttered under his breath, "Probably buried deeper in this facility."

Aris didn't respond. Her eyes stayed locked on the central terminal, jaw set. Ralik stepped back from the console, his visor dimming as the final log flickered out. The faint reflection of their faces lingered on the black screen, warped by its surface.

Just ahead, the corridor sloped toward a thick, sealed door plated in rust-streaked alloy. A red warning stencil was barely visible beneath the grime, partially scratched out, unreadable.

No guards. No checkpoints. No surveillance feeds alive this far down. Whatever this wing had been, no one wanted to come back to it.

Aris nodded toward it. "Let's see what they buried in there."

The lead-lined door hissed open with a reluctant grind, its rusted edges dragging against the floor like a warning. A gust of stale air hit them first. It was damp, earthy, and tinged with something chemical. Aris raised her hand, slowing the group's approach.

They stepped into a wide containment sector, ceiling arched like the belly of a buried ship. Roots bulged from the walls like veins under skin, pulsing slow and dim. The lights flickered in uneven intervals, illuminating rows of reinforced stasis pods lining the chamber. Some were intact, some shattered. Most were empty. But not all of them.

A low mechanical whir echoed from a nearby console as Ralik scanned the area. "This sector isn't abandoned. Power's still being routed here from somewhere else. Something kept these pods in cryo...until recently."

A wet, dragging sound cut across the chamber. From behind one of the broken pods, a figure lurched forward. Then another. And another. Each one towered over the crew...Olyssian soldiers reshaped by the very energy they sought to control. Their skin was marbled with bark-like plates and veined fungus, muscles wrapped in thorny vines that flexed unnaturally. Where their eyes once were, glowing amber pits burned dimly. One's jaw hung slack, with strands of root coiling through its mouth like a gag.

Fen took a step back, nearly tripping. "Those aren't soldiers. They're something else now."

"No," Thorne said grimly, raising his fists, "they're weapons."

The closest mutant gave a roar that sounded more like a broken windpipe than a battle cry...and charged. Aris barely rolled aside as it smashed into a console, shattering metal and sending sparks across the floor. Another lunged for Ralik, who swung his baton hard into the mutant's side. The strike landed with a dull thud, but the creature didn't even flinch. The creature swiped with a jagged, root-armored limb and slammed him hard into a wall. His visor cracked as he hit the floor. Thorne rushed to intercept, activating his gauntlets just in time to form a broad, humming shield between the crew and the charging brute. The mutant slammed into it with impossible force as its thorned limbs dug in, vines coiling over the edges like living wire. For a heartbeat, the shield held. Then it *cracked*.

The energy sputtered as the brute roared and surged forward again. The impact shattered the barrier with a shriek of broken tech. Thorne was launched backward, his body skidding across the floor before slamming into a support beam. He let out a strangled grunt and didn't rise right away...his arm bent at a wrong angle.

"Thorne!" Fen shouted, turning to run toward him just as one of the creatures lunged from the side. It caught him in the ribs with a bone-hardened limb, flinging him into a bank of flickering control panels. Sparks burst as he crashed through them, crumpling in the debris with a wheeze.

"Fall back!" Aris yelled, spinning on her heel as another mutant roared behind her. She fired off three sharp rounds into its chest, but it didn't even slow down.

"We can't take them head-on!" Ralik growled, trying to drag Fen upright while his own visor blinked with damage alerts. "They're too strong!"

One by one, battered and bleeding, the team fought their way toward the corridor, each of them limping, staggering, or dragging the other. Aris stayed back, firing controlled bursts to cover them, until Pixo managed to hit the corridor control and slam the reinforced door closed behind them.

Panting, hunched against the corridor wall, the team looked like shadows of themselves. Blood streaked from Fen's side. Thorne's gauntlet was sparking, his shield generator completely fried. Ralik's visor was cracked, and Aris's lip was split.

Pixo, the only one still moving cleanly, paced near the wall rack lined with sealed vials of Root concentrate. His tail flicked once, then twice as he studied the glow in the glass with a curious and calculating glance. Without a word, he grabbed one and held it up to the dim light, the violet liquid swirling like smoke inside.

"Well," he said, ears twitching, "we're clearly not winning on charm and good looks."

He turned, flashing a sharp-toothed grin. "So, what if we give our weapons a little upgrade? See how these pretty toys like a boost."

*The hum of old generators filled the corridor, punctuated by the soft clink of metal and the occasional hiss of torn med-patches.*

A soft overhead glow pulsed in rhythm with the root-veined walls, dim and irregular. It was like the planet itself was catching its breath. So was the crew.

Ralik sat with his back against a bulkhead, repairing the crack in his visor with steady hands, though the tension in his shoulders told a different story. Fen lay nearby, shirt removed, and ribs wrapped in a makeshift compression bandage, grimacing with every breath but still cracking the occasional crooked smile.

Thorne sat quietly off to the side, stripped down to the waist, one arm limp at his side while he tried to adjust the singed wiring in his gauntlet with the other. His torso was marked with bruises, burns, and fresh cuts, but beneath it all, a physique built like a fortress.

Aris approached him with a medkit and a glare that softened only slightly. "Stop fussing with it. You're not fixing anything like that."

He grunted. "Just trying to get it usable before next round."

She knelt beside him, unzipping the kit and pulling out a gauze spool and biofoam injector. "Hold still."

Thorne obeyed, exhaling slowly as she dabbed the foam along his broken arm. Her hands were steady, but her gaze flickered...just briefly to the shape of his chest and the way the muscles tensed beneath her fingers. Heat flushed across her cheeks before she caught herself and focused again.

"You're built like a reinforced hull," she muttered, not quite under her breath.

Thorne raised an eyebrow. "Was that a compliment?"

"I said hold still," she snapped, but it came out too soft to sound convincing.

Thorne let out a low chuckle, then winced as the movement pulled at the wound. "Remind me not to take compliments from you when I'm bleeding."

Aris rolled her eyes, but her hands didn't falter. "If I wanted to compliment you, you'd know."

"Uh-huh." His tone was casual, but his eyes stayed on her a second longer than necessary. "You always this gentle with your crew, or am I special?"

"You're lucky I didn't jab the injector into your lung."

Thorne smirked but said nothing more, letting the silence stretch between them, comfortable but charged. Aris taped down the last of the dressing and sat back slightly, her hands resting briefly on her knees.

For a moment, neither moved. The sounds of the others murmuring nearby, the faint clinking of metal and soft hum of power cells, filled the background. She could hear Ralik calibrating his visor, Fen muttering curses under his breath while checking his own gear. But here, between them, it was quieter.

"You're reckless," Aris said finally, voice low.

Thorne's gaze dropped to the floor, then back up. "You've always known that."

She nodded once. "And dependable."

His brow furrowed slightly, as if unsure how to respond.

She stood, closing the medkit with a snap. "Try not to break anything else. We're short on biofoam."

Without waiting for a reply, she turned and walked toward Pixo, her stride brisk, but her heart beating harder than she'd admit.

Behind her, Thorne watched her go, flexing his bandaged arm with a small grunt. "Reckless," he muttered, a small smile tugging at the corner of his mouth. "Yeah, maybe."

While the others patched up and rearmed, Pixo crouched at the far end of the chamber, surrounded by scraps, torn plating, and a pile of humming Root vials glowing faintly violet.

His tail flicked with rhythmic focus, ears twitching to the occasional spark as he worked. A makeshift workbench had been cleared with a broken crate turned sideways, covered with stripped gauntlet shells and exposed circuitry. His paws moved quickly, claws glinting as he rewired one of the pulse rifles and slid open a cartridge chamber.

"Pixo," Ralik said, stepping up behind him. "You're quiet. That usually means you're either onto something or about to blow something up."

"Please," Pixo scoffed, not looking up. "Only one explosion today. Two, max."

He inserted a root vial into a modified housing slot, twisting a copper wire around the chamber to stabilize the energy flux. The device hissed, then emitted a soft pulse. The violet light didn't flicker...it stabilized.

"Ha!" Pixo grinned, sharp teeth flashing. "I knew it would work."

Thorne approached, gingerly flexing his newly bandaged arm. "What did you do?"

"Integrated the Root concentrate into your shield emitter," Pixo replied. "Should generate a reactive burst on impact."

He handed the gauntlet over, then turned to Fen. "You, my overly optimistic friend, now have a plasma thrower that'll arc into anything rooted in this mess. You're welcome."

Fen blinked. "I didn't even ask for that."

"You didn't need to. Genius anticipates." Pixo paused in front of Ralik, visor flickering faintly as the strategist examined the modified gear on the others.

"For you," Pixo said, holding up a wafer-thin chip etched with shimmering Root circuitry, "I made something a little...cerebral."

He slotted it into the side of Ralik's visor, fingers moving with delicate precision. The display pulsed once, then fractured into new grids of scrolling data, arcs of spectral root energy, and faint predictive lines trailing movement paths.

"Layered pulse-vision, upgraded," Pixo explained. "You'll now see energy interference patterns, heat traces, impact trajectories...even anticipate motion paths based on kinetic drift. Short-term predictive readouts."

Ralik blinked behind the lens as new waveforms slid into view. His eyes tracked a faint afterimage of Thorne's gauntlet movement in reverse, a ghostly trail following his idle motion.

"This is...advanced," Ralik muttered.

Pixo shrugged. "You're the brain of this group. I figured it's time your visor caught up with your head."

Thorne chuckled from across the room. "So now he gets to know when we will screw up *before* we do it."

Pixo turned to Aris last, holding up her twin pistols. They gleamed, sleek and deadly, but subtly altered. Root conduits now laced along the barrel, and a low thrum pulsed from a crystal chamber nestled beneath each grip.

"For our fearless Firestarter," he said with a proud flick of his tail, "dual-channel energy cores. You've got split-mode functionality now, tap the trigger for standard bursts, or hold for a concentrated discharge that'll melt through alloy."

He flipped one in his hand before offering it grip-first. "Also synced the targeting system to adjust mid-fire. The more pressure you apply, the tighter the recoil damping. Basically, the pistols learn with you."

Aris turned one over, studying the soft violet glow running beneath the plating. It felt more alive and responsive, almost like it was waiting for her to move first.

"Try not to fire both charges at once unless you really hate something," Pixo added, stepping back. "Or unless you want to go flying backward into a wall."

She holstered them with a smirk. "No promises."

The next chamber offered no warning. The moment the doors groaned open, the enemy was already hulking, twisted, and waiting.

Aris led the charge, both pistols glowing with amplified resonance. She moved like a storm dispatching precise and unrelenting bursts. Each shot punched through armor and root alike, the impacts laced with concussive force that left craters in the walls behind her targets.

"Left flank!" Ralik called out.

"I see it," she snapped, twisting mid-step and double-tapping a lunging brute in the neck. It dropped before it could scream.

Thorne stepped into the chaos like a walking fortress. His power gauntlets thrummed with Root-fed charge, shields flickering to life with every incoming strike. A soldier lunged and Thorne met it with a heavy right hook, shattering bone and root in a single blow. Another came from behind. Without turning, he activated a reverse-blast, sending it flying with a flare of red energy.

"I can get used to this," he said with a slight smile.

Fen darted through the fray, his upgraded rifle humming with Root resonance as he fired burst after calculated burst. Each shot struck with pinpoint force, leaving arcs of seared root and shattered armor. The rifle's interface glowed along his forearm, reacting to his rapid targeting. One soldier lunged from the shadows, but Fen didn't flinch. He pivoted, dropped to one knee, and fired a charged round that sent the attacker sailing backward in a spray of violet sparks.

He popped up, eyes wide with excitement. "I don't know what Pixo fed this thing, but I owe him dinner."

From behind a pile of shattered conduit, Pixo's voice chimed in with a smug purr, "Make it two courses and dessert. I don't forget promises."

The last super soldier collapsed with a ground-shaking thud, vines twitching as the Root energy flickered and died in his veins.

Aris lowered her pistols as smoke curled from the barrels. Ahead of them, the chamber narrowed into a reinforced bulkhead with obsidian alloy inlaid with Root lines, pulsing faintly like veins beneath a scar. A half-burned Olyssian seal was stamped near the top, the rest too scorched to read. The panel beside it blinked with soft amber light, waiting for someone to make the next move.

Ralik's visor glowed faintly as he scanned the panel, the lenses flickering through spectral overlays. He placed a hand against the wall beside it, brows tightening. "There's a residual trail," he murmured.

"Energy signature...it's stronger here. Same frequency as the Root vials. It's leading down."

Aris stepped forward, her gaze following the sealed door. "To the Heartspire?" This wing wasn't abandoned by accident. It was sealed to keep whatever was down here from ever being found again.

Ralik gave a single nod. "Whatever they're chasing, it's close. This path is active."

With a few precise gestures, the visor pulsed in sync with the panel. The lock gave a heavy click, gears shuddering as the door creaked open, releasing a gust of stale, mineral-rich air. They stared into the black beyond, a hollow stairwell diving deep into Velmora's core.

Thorne stepped beside Aris, peering into the dark. "You'd think the Olyssians would install better lighting in their secret stairways to doom."

Pixo wrinkled his nose, his tail flicking. "Guess subtlety's cheaper than safety."

Fen adjusted his grip on his rifle, eyes scanning the threshold. "Only one way through now."

Aris didn't answer right away. She stared into the abyss, where faint pulses of violet light shimmered far below...like the slow throb of something breathing. She drew her weapon. "Then we keep going."

Without another word, they began their descent, boots echoing on cold metal, the pulsing glow below pulling them onward like a heartbeat in the dark.

# Chapter 7

## SPIRE AND SACRIFICE

The door groaned and shut behind them, sealing the route back with a hollow clunk of finality. Whether it locked or not didn't matter. None of them were going back.

The crew descended in cautious silence, boots echoing along the narrow stairwell spiraling deeper into Velmora's core. The walls shimmered faintly with embedded veins of crystalline root, their glow shifting from violet to emerald as they descended, an eerie signal of proximity to something ancient and untouched.

No one said aloud what they all understood: **the mission had changed**. This wasn't about mapping infrastructure anymore. Not about gathering data or clean exits. They were in it now. Buried in it.

And yet, none of them stopped. Whether it was loyalty, fear of turning back, or sheer stubborn momentum, they followed Aris down.

For Aris, the silence pressed hardest. She didn't regret bringing them here. Not yet. But she felt the weight of their trust like a lead weight in her chest. Every step forward was a gamble she hadn't intended to make when this started. Tavarin's orders were behind them now. Ahead was only what the Olyssians tried to keep secret.

She didn't know if she would find answers. But she knew she couldn't leave without trying.

It took several long minutes to reach the last step, and the cavern opened like a breath held too long. An enormous underground expanse stretched before them, aglow with a natural brilliance. Jagged gems the size of carts jutted from walls and ceiling, their refracted light bathing the hollow in shifting hues of blue and green. Woven through the stone like arteries were massive root structures, pulsing with a serene luminance. And in the very center, cradled by a shallow, glass-clear pond, stood a lone tree.

It was small, only a few meters tall, but unlike anything they had seen. Its bark shimmered like polished ivory, and its leaves glowed softly with an internal light, rustling in an unfelt breeze. Its roots extended outward into the water, where the pond reflected not only the tree, but what seemed like glimpses of memory and motion, events flickering just out of reach.

"Is that it?" Fen whispered.

Aris stepped closer. "The Heartspire?"

They barely had time to take in the sight before the air shifted. From behind the tree, a figure emerged, a tall being robed in flowing threads of living bark and crystal strands, eyes like blooming moss. Its voice echoed, deep and resonant, neither male nor female.

"You have come far. Not as thieves, but as seekers. Few do."

The crew instinctively stepped forward, forming a half-circle as the figure continued.

"I am the Guardian. I protect the Heartspire. It is not a weapon, nor a gift freely given. To take it is to claim power not meant for conquest. The Heartspire is the pulse of Velmora. Remove it, and the planet dies. Slowly, surely."

Ralik adjusted his visor, scanning the area. "Why would anyone do that?"

"Because they believe power justifies loss. Such is the nature of most beings. The invading beings have tried and failed to access the heart for many years. The heart was revealed to you because you don't seek its power. But once open, others may follow. That is the price of trust."

Before Aris could ask more, the ground trembled. A distant echo thundered through the cavern. The pounding of boots and the clatter of gear ricocheted off the walls, growing louder with each second. Commander Tavarin's sharp and cold voice preceded her.

"Move aside. That relic belongs to the Olyssian Accords."

Aris stepped between her team and the Heartspire. "You don't know what you're doing. You'll kill the planet."

"Then it dies," Tavarin snapped. "We have our orders."

The Guardian's form rippled, its limbs extending in sharp fractal patterns. Roots tore from the ground in a defensive snarl, coiling between Tavarin and the Heartspire. Energy pulsed, a wall of living light.

"You must not!" the Guardian thundered. "You awaken ruin!"

Aris lunged forward, firing. Her shots sparked harmlessly off Tavarin's shield. Thorne moved to block the soldiers, but the Olyssians overwhelmed him, forcing him back with brute force and riot batons.

Tavarin didn't hesitate. She drew a small blade, humming with the same frequency as the root veins. A device designed for this exact theft. A bypass tool, not brute force.

She sliced through the protective barrier. The Guardian's form cracked, shuddering as its defense failed.

In one swift motion, she placed her palm to the center of the tree and removed its heart. A pulse of golden-green light flashed, then recoiled. The leaves dulled. The roots coiled in on themselves. The pond went still, darkening to black.

The Guardian screamed. Not with sound, but with force. Its body shattered like splintering wood, twisting upward, reforming as something monstrous. Roots curled into spines. Limbs extended, gnarled and massive. A beast of bark, bone, and rage rose, screeching as the world around them cracked.

Tavarin's team fled toward their waiting ship, cradling the glowing Heartspire.

The cavern began to collapse.

"RUN!" Aris shouted.

The crew sprinted through falling debris, leaping over fracturing stone and ducking under plummeting shards of crystal. They barely made it to a loading tunnel, the planet above groaning in grief. When they reached the surface, Tavarin's ship was already breaking orbit.

Below them, the cavern ruptured open. From it, the newly corrupted Guardian was now a towering, planet-spanning beast, it emerged with vines tearing through cliffs and roots blotting out the sky.

"She doomed this world," Aris looked up, jaw set. "We must try to save it."

The creature's cry split the air, not just with fury, but with the agony of something ancient torn from purpose. Velmora itself seemed to shudder in protest, the wind thick with grief and ash. The crew stood in silence, hearts pounding, a moment of shared dread stretching thin.

Then, as one, they moved toward the impossible, toward the beast, toward the battle they chose to fight. The planet's last defense.

The wind howled across Velmora's broken surface, dust spiraling into the fading light as the monstrous Guardian loomed over the horizon. The once-holy creature, twisted by grief and stolen purpose, now resembled a titan made of roots and wreckage, stretching halfway across the landscape. Every movement it made sent tremors through the ground, its massive limbs tearing up stone like paper.

From a nearby ridge, the crew of the Zephira Dawn stared down at the beast.

"That thing...it's the size of a mountain," Fen muttered, awestruck and horrified. He gripped his newly-infused rifle tighter.

Aris scanned the terrain below, her voice measured despite the quake in her chest. "We can't let it reach any nearby settlements. The mines are already destroyed. We must limit casualties."

"We barely survived those twisted soldiers," Ralik added, adjusting the settings on his visor. "But if we fire from the Dawn we risk triggering a full collapse. The roots are holding this place together as much as they're strangling it."

Pixo leapt onto a boulder beside them, tail flicking. "Yeah, well...not like the Dawn's packing anti-titan weapons or can target as cleanly as us." He gave a sharp, humorless grin. "Looks like we're stuck doing this up close. Again."

Thorne activated the shield nodes in his gauntlets, the violet glow flaring to life. "Let's stop this thing. Together."

They descended the slope, each footfall bringing them closer to the impossible. The beast reared back, unleashing a roar that echoed across the broken plains. The force of it knocked trees flat and sent cracks spiraling through the rock. They weren't close enough to feel the full impact, not yet, but close enough to know what awaited them when they were.

Aris took point. "Hit the joints. Vines, roots, anything that looks like it moves. We must slow it down however we can. "

Once they were within range, Fen's rifle launched a volley of charged rounds, each burst hitting with a flash of purple energy. Thorne slammed his gauntlets into the ground, triggering a ripple that split the earth beneath one of the creature's feet, causing it to stumble. Ralik stayed at the edge of the battlefield, feeding tactical data through his visor.

Pixo darted between falling debris, launching small devices that latched onto the beast's limbs, emitting bursts of energy that disrupted its movements. "That one's for making me spill my rations, you ugly shrub."

The team fought with a coordination honed by desperation and trust. Still, the Guardian pressed forward, howling as its corrupted body bled purple ichor. The closer it neared the fractured canyon ahead, the more unstable the terrain became.

Suddenly, a surge of roots lashed out, sweeping across the battlefield. Aris shouted, "Scatter!"

They dodged but barely. Then, one massive root slammed into the ground just behind them, creating a shockwave that sent them flying. Pixo crashed hard, sliding across the dirt.

He groaned, rolling to one knee. "Still...not dead. But getting tired of saying that."

From above, the beast's core began to glow...an ominous signal that something worse was coming.

Aris, bruised and bloodied, looked to her team. "This ends now. We end it, or Velmora ends us."

But the momentum shifted. The Guardian slammed a colossal limb into the ground, tearing a deep scar into the battlefield and dividing the team. Ralik was cut off, Fen pinned beneath debris, and Thorne pulled Aris back just in time to avoid a sweeping blow.

"We can't hold this line!" Ralik called out. His visor sparked as it tried to maintain a tactical lock. "It's adapting. Learning. Our hits aren't slowing it down anymore."

Fen cursed from beneath the rubble. "We can't keep trading hits with this thing! We need another way to bring it down."

Thorne's shield sputtered as another wave of energy crashed over them. He grunted, chest heaving. "We're running out of time."

Pixo glanced from one wounded friend to the next, then looked up at the beast, its core now exposed, pulsing wildly with sickly purple light. "No...not out of time," he muttered to himself, then louder, grinning despite the sweat matting his fur. "Just out of options. Lucky for you, I've always been good at improvising."

Without waiting, he sprinted forward, weaving through chaos, clutching a small, custom-built device strapped tightly to his side. The others shouted after him, but he didn't look back.

Pixo climbed one of the jagged ledges, leaping higher than any of them could, agile and fast. He reached the Guardian's exposed core. Roots lashed out, but he dodged, slipping between them like smoke. At the top, he yanked a locking pin from the device, a compact explosive of his design, pulsing with purple energy, and slapped a palm to its ignition panel at his chest.

As he hit the device, Aris caught sight of it. Her eyes widened. "Pixo! Don't you dare! You won't make it out in time!"

"No one's allowed to hurt my crew but me," he said with a grin, then leapt into the air.

There was a burst of bright light as Pixo slammed into the Guardian's core, unleashing a shockwave of pure, cleansing energy. The explosion shattered the surrounding root shell, sending a blinding pulse across the battlefield. The Guardian howled, a deep scream echoing across Velmora's horizon. And then, for a long, still moment...silence.

The dust began to settle, curling in lazy spirals through the fading light. For a moment, none of them moved. The quiet descending on the world around them and echoed through their bones. The monstrous Guardian, once a titan of bark and malice, now lay crumpled in the canyon below. Its vast limbs twitched once, then stilled. The shriveled vines sloughed away in waves, their glow fading to nothing.

Aris stood first. Her legs shook, but she stayed upright, her gaze fixed on the smoldering crater where Pixo had made his final stand. She didn't speak. None of them did...not at first. The only sound was the soft wind, picking up ash like snow and sweeping it across the scarred ground.

"He did it," Fen whispered, his voice hoarse and cracked. He limped to Aris's side, one arm across his ribs, staring down into the blackened soil. "He actually did it."

Ralik stepped forward slowly, visor deactivating with a low hum. "That energy signature...it's gone," he confirmed. "Whatever link the beast had to the Heartspire was severed." His voice was hollow, more technical than emotional, as though stating the fact could help him process the reality.

Thorne dropped to one knee beside the edge of the canyon, scanning the broken stone. His expression was unreadable, locked behind grief and guilt. "I should've stopped him," he muttered, barely audible.

"No," Aris said quietly. "He made the call. Same one any of us would've made." She paused, her gaze never leaving the crater. "But he just made it first."

Another gust swept through, stronger this time, rattling loose stones and stirring the green-tinged air. From the heart of the crater, a faint shimmer began to pulse. A slow, rhythmic glow. It was gentle and steady and rose from the ruins, like a heartbeat.

The remnants of the Guardian's massive body began to shift. Roots uncurled, limbs folding inward as the corrupted shell collapsed in on itself. From the settling wreckage, a figure stepped forward. It was no longer monstrous, but the human-like form the crew had met before. The Guardian had returned, no longer twisted in its titan form, its bark-like skin etched with glowing green veins. Its eyes reflected sorrow, but also something calmer, more resolute.

"You have defeated my corrupted form," the Guardian spoke, its voice like wind through ancient branches. "At great cost."

Aris stepped forward, her voice tight in her throat. "He gave everything."

The Guardian bowed his head. "Though the Heartspire was taken, the corruption is undone. The roots will heal. Velmora will not wither. You have bought this world time to survive."

It raised its hand, reaching toward their weapons. One by one, they flickered with remnants of the corrupted energy still coursing through them. As the Guardian's pulse swept over the crew, that corruption vanished, replaced by a pure, vibrant green light. Thorne's gauntlets shimmered and stabilized, pulsing with protective force. Fen's rifle gleamed with precision, its rounds humming with new harmony. Ralik's visor blinked, coming alive with intricate patterns, his scans sharper, more connected to the world around him. And Aris...her pistols boomed with living energy, arcs of green light crackling from the barrels as if bound to her will.

"This is your gift," the Guardian said. "A blessing of balance. You fought not to take power...but to protect it."

A small gasp cut through the stillness. Floating just above the ground, shimmering like a mirage, was **Pixo**. His form flickered, his familiar feline silhouette outlined in soft, radiant light. His fur flowed with the wind, his expression relaxed in a small grin.

"Whoa," he said, glancing at himself. "Guess I clean up pretty well."

The Guardian smiled gently. "His spirit will not fade. Not here."

Aris blinked, stunned. "Pixo?"

He gave a casual wave, tail flicking with that familiar, irreverent energy. "I'll miss you Captain. All of you.

He glanced at Ralik with a grin. "And no, you're still not getting my tools."

The Guardian lowered its arm, and Pixo climbed onto its shoulder, settling in like it was the most natural thing in the world.

"The path ahead is not yet finished," the Guardian said, glancing past them toward the stars. "I can sense the Olyssians are moving toward the volcanic world of Ignarok. It is a place where fire and stone guard the next heart. Follow them. You will learn of the consequences that this galaxy faces if they are able to gather more hearts."

As it turned, its form shimmered with green mist. Pixo gave one final salute, eyes wide, grin intact. "Don't mourn too long," he said with a crooked grin. "I've got front-row seats now...and I better not see any of you screw it up."

And then they were gone. Only the wind remained, whispering through the broken canyon. The crew stood still, their weapons now gleaming with purity, the loss sharp in their hearts but tempered with something else, resolve.

Captain Aris holstered her twin pistols, her eyes heavy with tears. "Come on," she said, her voice hoarse. "We aren't finished. We can't let his sacrifice be wasted."

She knelt at the scorched ground, scooping a small handful of ash into the dented metal flask on her belt. The wind tugged at the rest, carrying it into the canyon. She sealed the flask, letting its weight settle against her side, and rose without another word.

# Chapter 8

## MEMORY AND MOMENTUM

The Zephira Dawn cut through the upper stratosphere of Velmora in solemn silence, its hull still scorched and streaked from the planet's violent reckoning. Below them, the once-lush world was reduced to dim glows and broken canyons. They didn't speak much, each member of the crew lost in the echoes of what they had just endured.

In the ship's main chamber, the atmosphere was quiet. No whirring tools from Pixo. No tail flicking by the engine room door. Just the low hum of the engine and the faint taps of Ralik's fingers against his datapad as he compiled a report for command.

Fen sat cross-legged near the viewport, staring out at the void with glassy eyes. "I never thought he'd go like that," he muttered. "I always figured if anyone could talk their way out of death, it'd be him."

Thorne leaned against the wall, arms crossed over his bruised chest, gaze unreadable. "He knew what he was doing. He chose it. For us."

Aris stood by the console, arms braced against its surface, her head bowed. The stillness that had once been companionable now felt suffocating. "He saved us. And he saved the planet," she said. "We carry that now."

Ralik looked up to the terminal. "Systems are stable. We are on auto-pilot to Planet Ignarok." His voice was steady, but his eyes kept drifting to the empty space where Pixo would've stood with some ridiculous quip.

A pause settled between them, heavier than before. Then Fen broke it, voice soft. "Do you all remember when he rewired the coffee unit to shoot foam darts at anyone who forgot to label their mugs?"

Thorne snorted. "I ended up dropping my favorite coffee mug because I was so caught off guard!'"

Ralik chuckled. "And that time he reprogrammed the training drones to dance instead of spar? We walked into the bay ready for drills and ended up watching synchronized bot ballet. He claimed it was a 'tactical morale boost,' but I caught him filming the whole thing for his secret comedy archive."

Aris allowed herself a faint smile. "He rigged my locker to explode glitter on my last birthday. It took a week to get it out of my boots. He said 'command presence' needed more sparkle. I nearly ejected him into space!"

Fen laughed lightly, leaning back. "He once pretended to be locked in the airlock just so I'd run diagnostics on the emergency override. When I opened it, he burst out wearing a cape made of emergency blankets. Said he was **Captain Meowgellan, Explorer of the Snack Sector.**"

"He was brilliant," Ralik added more quietly. "Creative in ways no one else dared to be. I never told him, but a few of my best modifications were just refined versions of his accidents."

They stayed there for a while, warm in shared memory.

Later that cycle, the crew gathered in the common area. A deck of well-worn cards slapped onto the table, leftover snacks collected from the storage bins. They played for fun without betting currency. Fen dealt while Thorne half-heartedly kept score with tally marks scratched into a datapad. Ralik played absently, still scanning background diagnostics, and Aris occasionally glanced from her cards to the viewport, lost in thought. It was peaceful and empty. Eventually, the others turned in, one by one.

Aris moved down the corridor toward the shower stalls, planning to retrieve the medscanner she'd left behind earlier during the crew's patch-up. It wasn't like her to forget gear, but the last few days had frayed every edge of her focus. As she turned the corner, she stepped straight into the humid air of the open stall and stopped cold.

Thorne stood there, towel slung low around his waist, chest glistening from the steam. He was drying his hair with another towel, clearly not expecting company.

Aris froze. "Sorry, I...I didn't know anyone was in here."

Thorne looked up, surprise flickering across his face before he dropped the towel from his hair. "No worries, Captain."

Her gaze betrayed her for half a second, darting over the sharp lines of his shoulders, the tattoos that curled down one bicep, and the solid muscles that flexed with even the smallest motion. There was strength in him, yes, but also something patient, like he carried the weight of the world and chose not to let it show. She blinked and turned on her heel, clearing her throat. "Right. I'll give you some space."

Before she could step out, his hand found her arm, firm but gentle.

She turned back. There was no hesitation in his eyes, only a gravity that pulled her in as he leaned forward. The kiss unfolded with breathtaking certainty, as though it had been blooming beneath the surface for months. His lips were warm, grounding her in the present and unspooling the tight coil in her chest. Her hand brushed lightly against his jaw, almost on instinct, anchoring herself in a moment that felt more like revelation than impulse.

Their kiss continued slowly, a cautious meeting of lips that quickly gave way to something deeper, more consuming. His kiss was full and soft, a striking contrast to the roughness of his usual demeanor. The touch of his mouth sent sparks fluttering through her chest. When his tongue met hers, she felt it as coarse, deliberate, searching, and it unraveled her composure completely. It wasn't just affection; it was hunger restrained, years of unspoken tension melting into something electric.

His hands, rough and strong, gripped her waist with surprising tenderness, then pulled her deeper with undeniable intent. Her fingers found his hair, damp and unruly, and she leaned in further, meeting him beat for beat as the kiss deepened. Time seemed to warp around them...there was no ship, no mission, just breath and contact and the pounding in her chest.

When they finally parted, her heart was racing, her lips tingling, and her skin still buzzing from the exchange. In that hush, she realized she had been craving that connection far longer than she ever let herself admit.

But reality pressed in like frigid air after warmth. She wasn't just anyone here, she was the captain. The crew's tether. The one who was supposed to lead, not falter. Not want things she wasn't allowed to have. The guilt twisted under her ribs.

"I..." she started, stepping back. "I'm sorry. This...we can't. Not yet."

Thorne didn't push. He didn't question. He gave her the smallest nod, his hand releasing her with a tenderness that made it harder to walk away.

She left without another word, but her fingers lingered at her lips.

The next morning, the crew reconvened. Ralik had just finished transmitting the report to the Interstellar Alliance Command: Velmora's near-collapse, Tavarin's theft of the Heartspire, every scan, every casualty.

The reply came through faster than expected, live and direct. The emblem of the command pulsed faintly across the screen before fading into the sharp-edged face of their operation's liaison.

"Your intel has been received and verified," the official said, voice clipped and efficient. "IAC was already aware of the Olyssian movements in this sector. Your mission remains unchanged: maintain pursuit, monitor Tavarin's movements, and collect further intelligence. Reinforcements will be dispatched, but given current fleet positions, it will take one week to reach your location."

Aris stepped forward, arms crossed. "One week's too long. By then, she could have destabilized another planet."

The liaison's expression didn't change. "Your orders stand. Continue observation. Do not engage unless necessary. Report all anomalies."

The transmission cut out before anyone could argue.

Thorne leaned back with a humorless snort. "Great. So, we chase her down and wait for permission to clean up the mess?"

Ralik's gaze stayed on the darkened console. "They've known about the Heartspire for months. They didn't tell us this in our initial intel briefs."

Silence followed, heavy with exhaustion and recognition that they weren't told everything.

Aris straightened, her voice quiet but firm. "It doesn't matter, I will not stand idly by and allow them to destroy planets or kill civilians."

She turned toward her crew, her gaze steady beneath the weight of everything they'd lost. "We take a moment. Then we prepare. Tavarin has the Heartspire. We can't let another planet fall."

Her eyes lingered briefly on the space where Pixo had so often stood. "We do this for him, too."

The others nodded. No one argued now. "Set course for Ignarok," Aris said. "We've got a job to finish."

# Chapter 9

## PIXO S POSTSCRIPT #1

**H**ey! Yeah, you! Don't go crying in your jumpboots just yet. I mean, sure. I made a big sacrifice, fireworks, heroic one-liner (still mad nobody wrote that down properly)...but come on. You think I wouldn't go out with style?

The truth is, I'm somewhere nice now. Really nice. There are trees that hum when you nap, snacks that refill themselves, and this hammock spun from starlight that sways perfectly.

So, keep going, crew. Keep fighting, keep laughing. And Aris? You were always my favorite. But don't tell Thorne. His ego's already the size of the Zephira.

Catch you next time!

— Captain Meowgellan, signing off.

# Chapter 10

## ECLIPSES OF EMBER

The Zephira Dawn pierced the atmosphere of Ignarok with a low, reverberating growl. Heat shimmered across the reinforced cockpit glass as flame-like clouds rolled past in molten swirls. Captain Aris Solene leaned forward in her seat, eyes scanning the horizon as the turbulence eased and the view below opened wide.

Ignarok was a world of harsh beauty. It was rugged and red, with sprawling obsidian plains etched by ancient lava flows. The terrain shifted in jagged contrasts: towering basalt cliffs cast long shadows over deep, glowing ravines, while scattered fields of scorched earth smoldered faintly like dying coals. Dust devils danced across the surface, casting trails of ash into the sky.

Out beyond the nearest ridge, they spotted clusters of life, humble villages clinging to survival like roots in volcanic soil. Mud-brick homes and Blackstone huts curled around natural hot springs, their glow pulsing like slow heartbeats in the dusk. There was no sign of a metropolis, just scattered pockets of habitation, each one built low and strong to withstand whatever this world threw at it.

"Where's the welcome party?" Fen muttered, squinting through the haze.

"They're probably hiding under rocks," Ralik replied, adjusting his visor. "Smart."

Aris's hands were steady at the landing controls. The Zephira banked gently and descended toward an open patch of land beyond the closest village. Steam hissed from the ground as the ship touched down, its hull already coated in ash by the time the engines cooled.

The moment the ramp lowered, the smell hit them. It was metallic, burnt, and strangely floral, like fire clinging to wilted petals. Aris motioned for the crew to stay sharp.

They didn't get far before the Olyssians found them. A patrol unit made up of four soldiers in tarnished black armor with glowing red visors crested the ridge with weapons raised. But before a fight could break out, a series of sharp whistles echoed from the village below. From behind weather-worn rocks and crumbled walls, locals emerged. Farmers, smiths, and elders who were worn but not broken surrounded the patrol in a sudden, silent standoff. One of the villagers, an older woman with silver-streaked hair and soot-dark skin, approached Aris.

"You're not one of them," she said. The crew's suits were able to translate her language automatically, smoothing the foreign cadence into something familiar.

Aris nodded. "We're not here to conquer anything. Just looking for someone." Their replies were also translated so that the villagers could understand them. Although, there seemed to be an understanding between them beyond words.

The woman's eyes narrowed thoughtfully. Then she raised her hand and just like that, the villagers turned on the Olyssians. A brief scuffle and a couple of blasts later, the patrol was disarmed, tied, and dragged away from sight.

"You've got more allies than you know," the elder said. "We've been under their boot for too long. And you...you carry the look of change."

Aris glanced to her crew, then to the village beyond. "We appreciate the assistance. We would like to help. Tell us what you need."

The elder gave a small nod, her expression unreadable beneath the soot-streaked lines of age and resolve. She whistled once, and several younger villagers emerged from behind the huts, motioning silently for the crew to follow.

The path into the village wound between low stone dwellings and steaming vents that hissed softly from beneath the ground. Children peeked out from behind heavy rocks, curiosity flickering in their eyes. No one spoke until they reached a cluster of homes near a hot spring-fed pond, the steam curling lazily into the dusk.

"This will be yours while you're with us," the elder said, gesturing to a hut. "We don't have much, but what we have, we share. You'll find food and water inside. Rest if you need it. But not for long. The elders will summon you shortly."

Accepting hospitality here was as much about trust as necessity. They couldn't afford to insult potential allies. "Thank you," Aris replied.

As the villagers dispersed, the crew took in their surroundings. The homes were modest but warm, built into the stone itself and reinforced with weathered metal scrap. Inside, woven mats covered the floors, and soft-glowing stones embedded in the walls provided light. A faint scent of fireleaf and simmering herbs lingered in the air.

Thorne dropped his gear in the corner and let out a quiet breath. "Could be worse."

Fen kicked off his boots. "Feels like a sauna with walls."

Ralik paced once around the room before sitting, visor still active. "This place is layered in geothermal veins. We're standing on a web of energy."

Before Aris could respond, a low chime rang out from a hanging metal disk by the entrance. A robed figure stood waiting outside. He was younger than the first elder but bearing the same serious expression. "They're ready for you," he said.

The crew regrouped and followed him to a large circular chamber built into the hillside. It was a village council hall, with ancient carvings of trees, fire, and stone etched into the volcanic rock. Seven elders sat in a crescent, their expressions grim.

"You say you've come to help," said one, his voice deep and cracked with age. "We knew someone would come. The ones from the sky. The ones who walk with loss but burn with purpose."

"We thought the others were here to help but we were foolish to trust them." A female elder said.

The eldest rose and stepped to a stone slab. He traced a weathered hand over the etchings. The four planetary symbols surrounded a swirling mass at the center, where a fifth, darker symbol was carved. He tapped one of the planets, marked with jagged edges and small flames carved above it. "Ignarok, the Second Flame. Guardian of fire and stone resides within. We were entrusted with protecting its heart, **Pyronyx**, we call it. The Heart of Flame and Stone."

He shifted his finger to the far left, where vines and a small tree were drawn. "**Velmora**, First Root. The green heart once kept in balance...now disturbed."

The elder's finger hovered next over a symbol marked by waves, carved to resemble crashing tides. "**Oquelis**, the Third Current. Said to be protected by the Guardian of Tides, its heart remains hidden beneath ocean and pressure."

Finally, he touched a symbol etched with wind-swirl patterns and four pointed spires. "And **Skyrend**, the Fourth Breath. Few remember its true form...only that its skies never sleep, and its guardian rides the storm itself."

He stepped back, his hand lingering over the center symbol, the one surrounded by the four. Unlike the others, it wasn't shaped like a planet. It was jagged, chaotic. Almost...starborn.

"It was never meant to awaken," he said, his voice low. "This...this is **Threxion**. The Celestial Carrion King. A god cast from the stars, sealed beyond the black veils of time. It ruled long before our worlds bloomed, and it fed on the light of creation. Only by dividing the hearts of the galaxy: roots, flame, tide, and wind, was it bound in sleep."

Another elder leaned forward. "But the old writings warn: should all four be drawn together again...its prison will break. And the stars will bleed."

The female elder nodded solemnly. "The ones who wear the mark of the Olyssians believe they seek power. But power is not what they'll find. If they claim all four hearts, they will not rise as gods...they will serve one."

Aris looked to her crew, jaw tight. "Tavarin already stole the first heart."

The room fell into tense stillness.

"Then time grows short," the eldest said. "And the shadow of *Threxion* grows longer."

# Chapter 11

## SANCTUM OF SMOKE AND STONE

**T**he stone chamber fell silent after the elders' final words. The symbols carved into the slab glowed faintly in the torchlight, and the shadow of Threxion seemed to stretch beyond the carving, seeping into their thoughts like smoke. Torchlight trailed behind them as they were led away, the air thick with the weight of unspoken consequence.

Outside, the village welcomed them with quiet nods and small gestures of hospitality. The Olyssian patrol had been neutralized, and for the first time in a long while, the villagers moved freely without fear. Children peeked around corners, curious but shy, while elders shared warm bowls of spiced root stew with the crew.

As they settled in, the elders approached Aris. "You must take the path to the Guardian. You will need his help. But the path to him will not open until the sun touches the peak of Emberwatch," one said. "Tonight, rest. Even the fiercest flame needs fuel."

That evening, the crew gathered near the geothermal springs nestled at the village's edge. The steam curled into the night like whispered prayers, and the waters carried a calming warmth that seeped into their bones. It wasn't peace, not truly, but it was a moment to breathe.

Aris found herself standing at the edge of the springs, steam rising in gentle clouds above the stone pools. The waters shimmered under the early moonlight, laced with subtle hues of amber and teal from the volcanic minerals beneath.

Fen and Thorne had already stripped down to their undershirts and slid into the water with groans of relief. The water soothed their aching pains and injuries. Thorne felt his arm was almost healed now.

Aris wandered a little farther from the group, her thoughts cloudy as the rising mist. The elder's words still echoed in her mind, threads of truth and myth woven too tightly to pull apart. She wasn't sure what disturbed her more: what they'd learned, or how much they still didn't understand. What else had command withheld? What else had been buried, rewritten, or reshaped to fit a narrative? She didn't doubt the threat, not after what they'd seen. But the full scope of it felt bigger than any briefing could've prepared them for.

Just beyond the springs was a grove of luminous flora, softly glowing under the touch of volcanic minerals. There, away from the noise, she spotted Ralik. He wasn't soaking in the water or relaxing like the others, he was crouched beside a young villager, refitting a broken mechanical splint on the boy's leg.

The child's mother stood nearby, wringing her hands until Ralik gently reassured her with a calm nod. He tightened the hinge with a tool from his kit, then adjusted the straps with careful precision. When he was done, the boy stood and tested the brace with only a slight limp. The mother bowed deeply in thanks before ushering her son back toward the village.

Aris stepped forward, drawn by the quiet tenderness of the scene. "That was very sweet of you, Ralik."

Ralik stood and offered her a modest shrug. "It didn't feel right not to. He reminded me of someone I knew once. Couldn't leave it undone."

She tilted her head, intrigued. "You're always the one looking out for everyone else. Sometimes I wonder...who does that for you?"

He smiled softly, and there was something in his expression...a vulnerability that rarely surfaced.

"Maybe I've just learned that helping others makes the weight of the world easier to carry. Doesn't mean it's any lighter, though."

She chuckled gently. "That sounds like something Fen would say...if he were pretending to be wise."

Ralik laughed, the sound light but sincere as he brushed a hand through his dark hair. "You're probably right. But maybe there's wisdom in pretending sometimes. Even Fen surprises us now and then."

Aris glanced sideways at him, her brow relaxing. "You surprise me too."

"Is that a good thing?" he asked with a gentle smile, eyes searching hers.

"I think...it is," she admitted, her voice barely more than a breath. There was a pause where neither moved. The space between them felt charged, not with tension, but with something quieter, deeper. Aris opened her mouth to say more, but words failed her.

The pressure of holding the team together pressed harder than ever, the weight of every choice, every loss settling deep beneath her ribs. She shouldn't feel this fragile. Not now. Not here. But guilt sharpened beneath the exhaustion, twisting with the ache she hadn't given herself permission to feel. They needed her steady. Unshaken. Unbreakable. And yet, tonight, she wasn't sure she was any of those things.

"You don't always have to hold everything together, you know," Ralik said quietly. His dark eyes stayed steady on hers, calm in a way that made it harder to hide from the truth. "Even leaders deserve moments to fall apart. Or to be cared for."

Her eyes met his then, unsure but open, caught in the vulnerability he offered and the strange pull it stirred inside her.

They stood in the stillness for a moment. Then, without saying anything else, Ralik reached up and unclasped a small crystal pendant from around his neck. He placed it in her hand. "This was given to me by a village healer on a world I helped long ago. It's meant to promote clarity and courage. You...might need both soon."

Aris looked at the stone, then at him. "Thank you."

He nodded, but his gaze lingered. His face had clean lines along his jaw and his smile shone perfectly, she hadn't let herself acknowledge it until now. There was warmth beneath his quiet exterior, the way he looked at her like she wasn't just a captain holding herself together. And before she could ponder longer, he leaned in.

The kiss began like a whisper...not urgent, but exploratory, deliberate. Ralik's lips brushed hers with reverence, as if he were afraid to steal something sacred. Then, slowly, he deepened it, not with hunger, but with devotion. His hand slid gently to her waist, the other ghosting up to cradle her cheek. His touch wasn't forceful, but enveloping, like being wrapped in warmth after a cold trek through the void. It was a kiss of patience, of feeling seen, Aris felt her breath catch, not from shock, but from how profoundly safe she felt. This wasn't the fire Thorne ignited, all storm and spark, this was something quieter, something that stirred her deeper. And it terrified her.

When they finally parted, the moment hovered between them like mist. Aris turned her face away slightly, breathing in the still night air. "We should get some rest. Big day tomorrow."

"Yeah," he replied, voice quiet. "Big day."

She walked back toward the springs, her mind swirling with questions she couldn't yet answer. Behind her, Ralik stayed in the grove, eyes lost in the firelit dark.

As the steam rose to meet the stars, Aris let the gentle calm guide her steps. Her thoughts wandered to the fire in Thorne's touch, to the devotion in Ralik's, to the impossible weight of wanting them both. Each stirred something different in her: passion and safety, wildness and calm. Two halves of a heart not yet whole.

She exhaled slowly, her chest tight with more than just fatigue. The night gave no answers, only the soft echo of footsteps as she returned to the water's edge. She was alone now. She felt the warmth of the water as she submerged her skin, allowing it to envelope her, embrace her. Her body felt weak, but the steam gave her comfort and, thankfully, time to think.

At dawn, the elders returned. The rising sun crested the jagged peaks of Emberwatch, its rays piercing through the veil of morning mist. When the first light touched the stones, it stirred the old energies beneath the earth, opening the path ahead. Soft golden light bathed the village, and a faint tremor rumbled beneath the earth.

"It is time," one elder said. "The path has opened. We will not be able to help you beyond this point. May the stars grant you strength."

The crew gathered their gear and followed the elders through a narrow trail carved into the volcanic ridges. The terrain shimmered with veins of molten glass and streams of slow-moving lava that wound like living arteries through the stone. Despite the danger, there was beauty in the terrain...glowing obsidian formations arched overhead like cathedral vaults, and delicate fireflowers bloomed in pockets of ash, their petals catching the light with an iridescent glow.

The deeper they went, the more surreal it became. Steam hissed from venting fissures, giving off a sulfur scent. Heat shimmered in the air like waves over desert sand. The path finally carved around a jutting ridge and emerged onto a high cliff ledge overlooking a vast lake of molten lava. The lake roiled and churned, casting a hellish glow across the obsidian cliffs and jagged stone pillars that ringed the basin. Rivers of fire cut through the terrain below like glowing veins, and bursts of pressure sent columns of flame spiraling into the sky. Above, smoke drifted lazily in the thick air, tinted red by the reflection of the lava's light. The oppressive heat pushed in on them, but the sheer awe of the landscape stole their breath. It was a haunting fusion of destruction and grandeur.

And then, he appeared. The Guardian of Fire and Stone rose from the lake of lava, his colossal form ascending through a geyser of molten flame. He stood twice the height of a man, sculpted from obsidian and living magma. Lava coursed through the cracks in his body like glowing veins, pulsing with ancient energy. His shoulders smoldered, smoke curling from the jagged edges, and his eyes burned with deep amber light, holding the weight of forgotten epochs. A crown of blackened stone and ember-crusted crystal circled his head, glowing faintly with each breath.

The crew instinctively paused, standing at the edge of the cliff, awed by the sheer presence before them. The heat swelled with each step he took, but none of them moved.

"I am Pyronyx," the guardian's voice boomed, echoing across the cliffside and the volcanic basin below. "Flame-born sentinel. Brother to the Root."

He looked directly at Aris. "I know why you have come. The Guardian of Velmora passed word of your mission. The Heart has been taken. And still, you come seeking another."

Aris stepped forward. "We don't seek to steal your heart. We only want to stop the Olyssians."

Pyronyx studied her for a long moment, then the rest of the crew. "Words are wind in the forge. Intent must be proven. Purpose must be tempered."

He gestured, and the lake flared with sudden brilliance. The air thickened, pressing down on them like a furnace. "If you claim the blessing of flame and stone, then step forward. Not as warriors but as souls willing to burn. Each of you must walk your own path, face what haunts you, and rise anew."

The cliff beneath them cracked and shifted, revealing multiple spiraling obsidian paths leading downward toward the heart of the lava basin.

Joseph Young

"Enter the Crucible," Pyronyx intonated. "Let the Trial of Fire begin."

# Chapter 12

## PIXO S POSTSCRIPT #2

Turns out dying gives you excellent front-row seats to the dramatic mess your crewmates keep hurling themselves into. From here, I get to watch it all like an interstellar soap opera. Honestly, 10/10 afterlife experience.

Now, I get it. There's a galaxy to save. Ancient gods to stop. Hearts of planetary elements to recover. All overly dramatic. But does the crew have to do it **while emotionally imploding**?

Let's talk Aris. Captain Command. Braver than a two-headed drake in heat, but right now? She's tangled in more romantic tension than a holonovel. You've got Thorne. He's brooding, battle-scarred, and about as subtle as a meteor punch. Then there's Ralik who is the soft-spoken fixer with eyes like he's permanently two seconds from a tragic poem. And she kissed them both? Girl. You can't just dual-wield feelings like that without triggering a cosmic love triangle event. Fen's probably fine. Emotionally bruised, deeply loyal, quietly carrying the whole squad's soul on his back...*standard Fen behavior.*

Anyway, they're about to dive into a trial of fire and hallucinations. Which is either a therapeutic breakthrough or the worst group retreat ever.

Me? I'll just be watching from my celestial window seat, snacking and placing bets on who cries first.

Your Friendly Former Fuzzball,

Now Streaming from the Stars

—Pixo,

# Chapter 13

## FURNACE OF THE FORGOTTEN

Darkness swallowed the crew the moment they stepped past the cliff edge toward the multiple paths. The heat hit first, it reached into their lungs, clawing through bone and thought alike.

Then, the cliff fractured. Not in an explosion, but slowly, unnaturally, like silk unraveling thread by thread. The path behind them vanished, replaced by a choking veil of smoke and shimmering flame. The sound of the elders grew distant until silence fell like a guillotine.

One by one, each of them vanished into their own flickering spiral of heat and shadow, pulled apart by invisible hands, their souls stretched across the crucible's hidden corridors.

Their trials had begun.

### Ralik Aeran

Ralik landed in a field of mechanical wreckage, ash and rust stretching for miles in every direction. The sky churned with oily clouds, static lightning flashing like fractured memories. The air pulsed with an unspoken grief, as if the very land mourned something unfinished.

At first, he wandered the wreckage, calling out for his crew. His voice echoed through the twisted remains of metal limbs and shattered hulls. Each time he called out, the metal reacted, dark red eyes following him as he walked past. Then, in the distance, he saw a tall woman, standing amidst the smoke.

"Taylor," he said, breath catching in his throat.

She turned. The gentle pull in her eyes, the quiet storm of memory behind her features. She was the first to reach inside the rusted parts of him and try to understand what lay beneath. And the first to abandon him when she saw too much.

Ralik approached, but with every step he took, the ground grew hotter, the air thicker. The wreckage around him started to melt, not from heat, but from something deeper...guilt, perhaps. Or longing.

"Always the fixer," Taylor said, her voice laced with venom disguised as silk. "Wires, circuits, broken engines. You tried to fix us. As if love was something you could solder back together."

Confused, Ralik stepped back. He opened a panel in the nearby wreckage, trying to distract himself with tools in hand, breath shallow. It had always been easier to repair a shattered circuit than face what he couldn't control.

"You didn't listen," she continued, stepping forward. "You smothered with care. You built walls out of kindness and never noticed when I stopped breathing behind them."

The wreckage hissed. Her voice was louder now, crueler. Her form shifted, her hands glowing with fire, her limbs jagged and sharp like forged iron.

"You think if you fix enough, if you give enough, you'll finally be worthy. But you hide inside that, don't you? You're terrified of being left again."

Ralik's tools sparked in his hands, but he couldn't fix this world. Every attempt made the world darker. The storm above grew angrier, the wreckage rising like twisted roots trying to entangle him. Taylor was gone. In her place stood a fire-drenched specter. Her rage, his guilt, their shared disappointment incarnate.

She lunged. He rolled away and gathered himself to his feet. She struck again, and again, her fists landing hard, each time his footing slipping further. She was faster. Stronger. And yet, with every blow, he saw less of her and more of his own reflection in the flames. He hid behind a warped panel, breathing hard, chest tight.

Then a memory surfaced, not Taylor's leaving, but what came after. The nights he stayed awake, rebuilding the same prototype repeatedly. He would do it to distract from the void she left behind and the ache he felt inside.

He stood slowly. This wasn't about her. It wasn't about proving himself to anyone else. This trial was about him. About letting go of what he couldn't fix, what he couldn't save. About moving forward anyway.

"You were never mine to fix," he said, voice shaking. "And I'm not broken for failing to keep you. I tried...not because I was weak, but because I believed in something. I believed love meant saving someone. But now I understand, it means letting them go. It means letting myself heal. And I still believe in that."

The specter paused. Her flames flickered. Then, slowly, her body cracked, like a shell splitting open.

She shattered into embers, drifting upward like fireflies. The wreckage softened. The ash settled.

Ralik stood alone, breath slow, hands open. Not healed. But free. And that was enough.

## Thorne Kaid

The heat folded around him like a vice, and when the blinding light faded, he stood once more within the steel veins of the prison, *Blackmarsh-7*. It hadn't changed much, not in his memory. The walls still sweated rust. The buzz of flickering lights still hummed above, and the scent of scorched metal and chemical disinfectant clung to the air like a stain that never quite washed away.

He hadn't been here in years, but the place still lived beneath his skin. He turned slowly, boots echoing against the grated floor, and saw them, the guards who had sneered at him like a wild dog behind glass. The other inmates, nameless now, all blurred behind walls of flame and steel.

Then he saw himself. A younger version, leaner, harder, eyes too sharp with pain and too dull with hopelessness. The man who'd just arrived at Blackmarsh, carrying the guilt of a choice made in desperation. The Thorne who had given up everything to save a family he didn't know and paid for it with years behind these bars.

"Do you remember this corridor?" the younger Thorne asked from across from him in their shared cell. His voice was hushed but steady, cutting like a buried blade. "Do you remember how it felt to be paraded down this hall? Shackled. Judged. Forgotten."

Thorne nodded but said nothing yet. He did remember. Every day. Every whisper behind the reinforced glass. Every time someone turned away when he entered a room. Even after his sentence was served, the walls followed.

"You did the right thing," the younger version continued, circling him now. "You saved lives. But in the end, what did it cost you? Your rank? Your future? Your name?"

He stopped in front of Thorne again, eyes narrowing. "And what did it gain you, really? Do you think the crew knows the full story? Think they'd follow you if they did?"

Thorne clenched his jaw, but the words didn't come easily. "I never hid it," he finally said. "I told Aris. I told the captain who brought me in. I never claimed to be a saint."

"Maybe not," the ghost replied, smirking. "But you still carry the scar, even if no one can see it. You still scan every glance for judgment. Still hear the chains, even when they're gone."

The walls began to shift. Cells stretched into infinity. The voices returned...taunting, mocking, accusing. From commanders who dismissed him to civilians who eyed him with quiet suspicion. The walls bore the weight of his past, and that weight pressed into his chest like stone. A voice rose from behind him, too familiar.

"You're not a hero, Thorne," it said. "You're just a man who crossed a line. And maybe you've been trying to make up for it ever since."

Thorne staggered back as a figure stepped from the shadows. It was not his younger self, but an Olyssian officer from his past. The one who turned him in. The one who let him take the fall. His old friend.

"You never said a word in my defense," Thorne muttered, the pain bleeding into every syllable. "You knew why I did it."

The officer shrugged. "It didn't matter. Orders are orders. You broke them."

The trial pressed tighter, the floor trembling beneath him. Fire licked at the edges of the corridor. The specters shouted louder, their voices an overwhelming tide of shame and memory. His lungs burned, but he stood his ground.

"Maybe I did break the law," he said, louder now, voice raw with truth. "But if I had to do it again, I would. I saved lives. That has to mean something."

The crowd of ghosts began to converge on him, shouting, reaching, demanding penance he'd already paid. His knees buckled as the heat rose, suffocating. For a moment, he thought he might sink into the floor, into the guilt, into the past.

Then he saw Aris. Not physically, but as a memory, standing firm at the helm, trusting him. He saw Fen's laughter, Ralik's calm gaze. The crew. They had seen the man he was now. Not the prisoner. Not the convict. Just Thorne.

"I carry it," he said, rising slowly. "The guilt. The regret. The label. I carry all of it. But I keep walking. I don't let it stop me anymore. That's the difference."

The flames began to dim. The walls cracked. The specters faltered, losing shape and form. One by one, they faded into ash, carried by a breeze that hadn't existed a moment before.

The corridor dissolved into molten rock and golden light, and Thorne stood alone again on his platform. He was bruised, sweating, his breath ragged. But standing.

### Captain Aris Solene

The obsidian path narrowed beneath her boots, its shimmering edges melting into molten light. With each step, the heat thickened, clinging to her skin like a second layer, drawing sweat from her brow and a weight from her chest. She squinted ahead, but the world blurred red, then shifted. The dark cliff faded, and a new scene emerged from the haze, forged by memory and regret.

She stood alone in a wide stretch of red sand, the sky overhead a burnt-orange expanse, dense with swirling clouds. There was no doubt. This was the mission site. The place where Samir died.

A figure moved through the heat shimmer ahead, his outline surfacing slowly like a ghost reluctant to return. He stepped into focus, tall, lean, wearing the same Olyssian field jacket with the half-zipped collar she'd once teased him about. One hand held his helmet loosely at his side; the other lifted in casual greeting. Samir. Just as she remembered him. Her breath caught, heart aching from the sudden rush of memory. He hadn't aged a day.

"That's still your look, huh, Solene?" he said, offering that same crooked smile that used to melt through her stubbornness. "Like you're ready to fight the whole galaxy."

She didn't answer right away. Her voice felt stuck behind everything she hadn't said to him. The years of silence, guilt, longing. "Samir..." she finally whispered.

He stepped forward, eyes glinting with warmth and something else, sadness, maybe. "You never stop, do you? Still throwing yourself into every battle. Still carrying the weight like it's yours alone."

She swallowed hard, unable to move. The way he looked at her twisted something inside. It was like her heart had been pulled back into that moment, the day she made the call that cost him his life.

"You're not real," she said, more to herself than to him.

"No," he replied, gently. "But your guilt is."

He circled her slowly, voice softer now. "You carry me like a blade in your side. You keep others out because you think letting them in will end the same way. You think if you care again, you'll lose again."

She turned to face him, eyes hard despite the tremble in her chest. "I made the decision. I gave the order that sent you in. I sent you to die."

"And I went," he said. "Because I believed in you."

The heat around them intensified. The air warped. Samir's form shimmered and shifted. His face changed. The angle of his jaw. The look in his eyes. Suddenly, it wasn't Samir standing there anymore...it was Ralik. But not the one she knew exactly. It was him, distorted slightly, more symbolic than real. The same gaze. The same calm depth. The same vulnerability.

"You see him in me," the figure said, voice now Ralik's. "The way I speak. The way I listen. The way I try to fix things, even when they're beyond repair. Just like he did. And look where it left him."

Aris stepped back, her hands trembling. She shook her head slowly. "This isn't fair. This isn't..."

"It's true," he cut in gently. "You want to let go. You want to feel something again. But you're terrified. Because if you do...and it breaks again...what's left of you then?"

She closed her eyes, breathing in the fire-drenched air. Everything felt suffocating. Her past, her fear, the aching truth of her emotions. She remembered the late nights she avoided sleep just to avoid dreaming. The way she deflected when Ralik looked at her too long. The way her heart squeezed when she thought of Samir, and how sometimes, somehow, it did the same with Ralik.

"You think honoring my memory means staying alone," the voice said. "But that's not love. That's fear wearing love's face."

The sand beneath her cracked. The air shimmered violently. Aris fell to one knee, overwhelmed by a flood of emotions . All the years she had hidden behind duty. Behind command. She let it all rise now. The guilt. The grief. The longing. And still, the hope.

It wasn't just losing Samir that had carved the hollow in her chest, it was giving the order that led to it. The weight of command had always demanded sacrifice, but she'd never expected to survive the cost. Loving someone again, stepping into that risk, meant facing the possibility that she might have to make that call again. Or worse, that when the moment came, she wouldn't be able to.

"I did love you," she said quietly. "And part of me always will. But I'm still here. I still feel. And maybe...maybe that's not betrayal. Maybe it just means I'm finally letting myself live."

The figure nodded once. The flames calmed. The distorted vision dissolved like smoke on the wind, leaving behind nothing but scorched sand and a single crimson flower blooming from a crack in the earth.

Aris rose slowly, heart heavy but no longer chained. She didn't leave the memory behind. She walked forward with it beside her.

## Fen Orlan

Fen stepped cautiously along the obsidian path, his boots clinking lightly against the smooth stone. Heat curled around his body like smoke, thickening until the cliffside melted away and the world collapsed into a red-tinted haze. As his vision steadied, the terrain took shape. It was a ruined village, one he hadn't seen in years, but which lived in the corners of his memory like an unhealed scar.

Burnt wooden beams jutted from the earth like broken ribs. Crumbled stone walls lay scattered in heaps, blackened by fire. The air smelled of ash and scorched earth, and the sky above was still, almost unnaturally so. There was no wind, no sound. Just stillness, oppressive and complete.

He turned slowly, already knowing what he would see. At the edge of the wreckage stood two figures, hand in hand, gazing out over what remained of their home. His mother's hair was braided just as it had been the night before the invasion. His father wore the same stitched family coat, the crest half-torn, threads fraying with time. Fen's breath hitched inside his chest. His throat closed tight.

They didn't turn to him. They didn't speak. They only stared ahead, still as statues. Then, the quiet broke with a sound that rolled like distant thunder. A tremor passed through the ground as boots struck stone. The soldiers came, emerging from the smoke like ghosts clad in red-lit armor, their helmets featureless, visors glowing like furnace glass. Olyssian.

Fen's chest tightened, the memory crashing into him before his thoughts could catch up. The soldiers moved without urgency, methodical in their approach. They surrounded his parents, and though he knew what came next, he still shouted and ran toward them, desperation thick in his voice. But the ground softened beneath him, the stone cracking like crust over lava. He dropped to one knee, then both, crawling forward as the heat stole his breath. A weapon was raised.

"No!" he yelled, reaching through fire and smoke and memory.

The blast struck. His parents disappeared in a flash of flame, just like they had in life. Fen screamed, knuckles white against the obsidian. He was too late. He'd hidden back then, watching helplessly from the rafters. And even now, when given the chance, he hadn't stopped it.

But this time, he walked towards them. The soldiers turned toward him, their movements mechanical, weapons glowing at the ready. He looked around for something, anything, but there was no weapon, no shield, no place to run. Just ghosts and regrets. He raised his fists out of instinct, muscles tensing. He was ready to fight this time, even if it meant losing.

Then, a voice stirred within him. "You never had a chance to save them. But you have the chance now...not to fight the past, but to face it."

The words steadied him. He took a breath and remembered how his mother used to speak of the flame trees that grew back after every wildfire on their home planet of Lutharia. Their roots were stubborn, but their leaves were brilliant. He remembered how his father said that real valor wasn't about being the strongest in a fight, it was about choosing to stand when everything told you to fall. Fen lowered his fists. The soldiers hesitated.

"I'm not afraid of you," he said, voice uneven but steadying with every word. "You're not real. You're just the shape of my pain."

He stepped forward. The ground held beneath him this time. The soldiers raised their weapons, but still, they didn't fire.

"I couldn't save them," he continued, each word scraped from the weight of years. "But I can carry them. I can fight for what they believed in...not because I'm angry, but because they taught me what it means to keep going."

The soldiers flickered. Their armor cracked. Slowly, they dissolved, not into smoke, but into light. Not erased but released.

Around him, the ruins shifted. The village no longer burned. Flame trees stood tall along the path, their orange-gold leaves glowing softly in the light. His parents stood beneath them one final time, no longer victims, but symbols, reminders of what shaped him. They didn't speak, but they didn't need to.

Fen straightened. His breath slowed. His gaze hardened with quiet resolve. He turned toward the path that now revealed itself, and took the first step forward, no longer burdened by the past but guided by it. He wasn't just the steady hand of the crew, he was its courage.

The spiral paths converged slowly, curling upward like molten veins along the cliff's edge. One by one, they emerged to where they started the trial...soot-streaked, sweat-soaked, and silent. No words passed between them at first. There was only the sound of their breathing, the hiss of nearby lava flows, and the distant, rhythmic pulse of Pyronyx's heart still beating within the volcanic basin.

Ralik was the first to lift his head. His eyes met Thorne's across the shimmering heat. Neither spoke, but something unspoken passed between them. Not comfort, not even camaraderie, but recognition. Both had walked through ghosts they hadn't named in years.

Fen arrived moments later, limping slightly, his hand pressed to his chest as if holding something invisible but sacred. When he saw the others, he didn't smile, but he nodded. He was firm, present, more grounded than before. His usual bright energy was dimmed, not diminished, shaped into something steadier.

Last was Aris. Her walk was slow, her expression unreadable. The heat curled around her like a second skin, but she didn't flinch. As she stepped onto the shared stone platform, her gaze swept over the crew, each of them marked by the fire in different ways. Thorne's shoulders carried more weight now, he felt he had earned his place as the crew's protector. Ralik's hands trembled from his emotional state, but he kept moving. Fen's jaw was set in quiet resolve. She exhaled once and took her place among them.

From the basin below, the lava stirred. Pyronyx rose once more, his massive form unfurling from the fire like a god reborn. His eyes glowed with molten clarity, and this time, his voice held something different, not challenge, but reverence.

"You have walked through memory, regret, and pain. Not as conquerors, but as truth-seekers. You have faced the fire within and found form in the flames."

He raised one massive hand, and from the pool of lava rose four shards of obsidian, each laced with glowing seams of orange light. The shards floated toward them, hovering in front of each crewmember.

"These are fragments of my flame," Pyronyx said. "Not weapons, but echoes of your transformation. Carried not to harm, but to remind. You are now stronger than who you were."

The shards pulsed once, then slowly embedded themselves into the crew's armor. It wasn't forced, the armor accepted them as if by choice.

"Thank you," Aris said, her voice low, steady. "For the fire. For the truth."

Pyronyx bowed his head, smoke curling from his crown like a crown of embers. "May you burn brightly, and wisely."

The cliffside trembled, and a path opened behind them of cooled obsidian, leading upward into the distance.

They walked together this time, without hesitation.

Touched by what had happened. But united. Forged.

# Chapter 14

## BLOODLINES BENEATH THE BLAZE

The ground trembled beneath their feet as the last of the obsidian paths sealed behind them. The trials were over, but the heat had not relented. Above them, Pyronyx watched in solemn calm from his perch high above the molten lake. The crew stood at the edge of the basin, weary. They had faced the flames and returned as tempered souls, each bearing the weight of their truths.

The shards of Pyronyx's blessing had embedded themselves into their armor, fragments of obsidian and molten crystal etched along seams and joints, each glowing faintly with protective energy. Its powers didn't make them invincible, but it made them more resilient, in body and in spirit.

Aris turned to face her crew. The words she carried were heavy, but they came with a gentleness that hadn't been there before. "I know we've been through so much together," she said, her voice quiet but firm. "I know what you've endured. And I know the trial wasn't just about heat or fire. We were each tested in the deepest parts of who we are. And we came back."

Her gaze moved from one face to another. "Not perfect. Not whole. But together. That matters more than anything."

She stepped forward and pulled Fen into a hug, brief but firm. " You keep us steady, even when everything else is falling apart," she whispered.

Next was Thorne. She wrapped her arms around him without hesitation. She allowed herself to feel the comfort of his muscular arms enveloping her, it felt like she could stay here forever. "Your strength is why we're still standing. You've always been our shield."

Finally, she turned to Ralik. For a heartbeat, they simply looked at each other. Then she stepped in and hugged him longer than the others. Her voice was quieter this time. "You always see more than you let on. And you carry more than you should. Thank you for staying."

When they pulled apart, Ralik simply nodded, his eyes holding his usual softness.

Before the moment could stretch too far, the ground beneath them shook. From the volcanic basin below, a deep groan rumbled through the earth. The sky darkened, clouds twisting into a spiral above the central volcano. Heat surged in unnatural waves.

"That doesn't feel natural," Fen muttered.

"No," Ralik said, checking his scanner. "This is something else."

Together, they climbed the ridge path again, reaching the cliffs that overlooked the core of the planet's volcanic heart. From this new vantage, something caught their eyes, a massive structure nestled at the base of the volcano. It hadn't been visible before but now stood clearly: a castle forged of black basalt and streaked with glowing red ore, pulsing as if in rhythm with the magma below.

"That wasn't there before," Thorne said grimly.

"Or it was hidden," Aris replied. "Either way, we need to check it out."

They descended quickly, weapons ready. As they approached, the air grew heavier, ash clinging to their skin, the scent of scorched stone filling their lungs. Olyssian soldiers stood around the perimeter, guarding the entrance to the castle. The crew moved behind a wall of jagged rock that was twenty meters away. But before they could plan an approach, the gates opened.

A voice echoed from within. "Let them in." Commander Tavarin stood in the courtyard, her armor reflecting the lava-light, helmet tucked under one arm. Around her, her soldiers stayed alert but did not raise their weapons.

"You're far from Velmora," Aris said.

"I've followed my orders here," Tavarin answered. Her face was hard to read, a storm of emotion behind her eyes. "But that's not the only reason I'm here."

Aris stepped closer. "What other reason do you have?"

Tavarin hesitated. "Because I went through the Crucible. It showed me something I didn't expect. Something I didn't even know I was looking for."

She looked directly at Aris, then lowered her voice. "I saw our father. I saw...us. Together."

Aris blinked. "What are you talking about?"

"We share the same blood," Tavarin said. "Same father. Olyssian explorer. I didn't believe it either, not until the vision. Not until the pain of knowing made it impossible to deny."

The air went still. "I'm not here to fight you, Aris. Not this time." Tavarin looked down, her voice trembling.

She swallowed hard, her gaze flicking to the fractured ground beneath them. "The Crucible didn't just show me pain. It showed me what I've become. What I've been complicit in. I thought I was serving something greater. I thought sacrifice made us stronger. But it doesn't. It just leaves graves behind. I can't pretend I don't see that anymore."

"But I can't abandon my mission either. My master...he's not just powerful. He's terrifying. If I fail him, I'm dead. If I succeed, everything burns."

Aris clenched her jaw, torn. It sounded impossible, the enemy who had hunted them now claiming to share her blood. And yet...some part of her wanted to believe it. Some part of her wondered if family meant anything at all anymore.

Tavarin stepped closer. "Join me. Please. We can stop this from the inside. We can survive. You and I. Together."

Ash drifted around them, silent as snowfall. Then the air changed, as if charged, crackling with invisible tension. A piercing hum echoed through the volcanic valley, followed by a pulse that reverberated through their bones. From the haze above, something descended. Not from the cliffs, but from the sky.

Through the thick swirl of ash, a dark vessel emerged. Its surface shimmered like blackened glass, smooth and sharp, etched with the insignias of Olyssian High Command. The craft hovered with an unnatural stillness before touching down outside the castle's edge. A ramp unfurled with a slow hiss, steam venting in all directions.

From the mist stepped a man. Clad in obsidian armor laced with gold ornate, his helm bore the shape of a serpent with curved fangs at the jaw. The symbol on his chest was different from the rest...no longer the standard military crest it marked him as an Olyssian Elite. The highest echelon of their forces. Untouchable. Unforgiving. Aris recognized it instantly. Where ordinary soldiers enforced, the Elite erased.

His gait was unhurried, almost regal, exuding a terrifying grace. Around him, even the Olyssian guards bristled with restrained fear. He hadn't come through the Crucible. Men like him didn't need to. The Elite had other ways in.

He carried a cane, smooth and dark as the void, but every step he took whispered of power. A dark ring gleamed on his hand, unassuming at first glance. When his fist lifted and aimed, a soundless pulse erupted forward. One soldier faltered, too slow to bow. A strangled gasp escaped him before he crumpled to the ground. No wound. No cry. Just collapse, his body destroyed from within as a gravity spike compressed the blood in his veins until his heart simply stopped.

Aris reached for her weapon instinctively, but Tavarin raised a hand. Her eyes widened with dread.

"Stand down," she said softly. "That's General Talos."

The name sent a chill through the crew despite the heat of the volcano. Stories of him were whispered like curses, an enforcer of the highest command, a tactician who favored control through crushing his enemies, and a man said to have never failed a campaign. The general stopped just inside the courtyard, the heat visibly warping the air around him. He removed his helm, revealing sharp, angular features and piercing eyes the color of forged steel. He scanned the scene, lingering on Tavarin and Aris.

"Commander Tavarin," he said, his tone quiet, dangerously even. "You were due to return to the fleet two days ago. I see now why you did not."

Tavarin stepped forward, hesitating for only a moment. "General, I can explain..."

He held up a hand. "No explanation needed. I saw it in your hesitation before. And now I see it written on your face. Compassion. Treachery disguised as mercy."

Aris stepped beside her. "She was only trying to protect me."

He turned toward Aris. "You have her face, you know. But you'll never have her loyalty."

Then, before anyone could move, he extended his cane, and the blade slid free with an elegant hiss. The obsidian shimmered like a black sun.

Tavarin's eyes widened. "No...wait!"

A single slice and in the blink of an eye, Tavarin dropped to her knees, coughing blood. Tavarin gasped as she collapsed, her knees hitting the blackened stone. Aris lunged forward, but too late.

Blood stained Tavarin's lips, but her eyes found Aris one last time. In that fleeting moment, they softened, not with pain, but peace. Her lips moved, barely a whisper, but Aris caught it: "I'm sorry." Then the light faded from her eyes, and she slumped forward, still and silent.

The General sheathed the blade into the cane and turned without ceremony. "Clean this up," he ordered the guards. "And ensure these intruders are dealt with. I have to continue the mission in her place."

Aris stayed there, the crew surrounding her in a hush, none daring to speak. The sister she'd only just found was gone. And something inside her had gone with her.

# Chapter 15

## PIXO S POSTSCRIPT #3

**W**ell, well, well...this one took a turn, didn't it? If you're reading this, then you probably watched the whole emotional landslide unfold from that lava-ridden castle, and yeah...I felt it too.

Even from where I'm watching, everyone here is starting to freak out! I saw the Guardian of Velmora spit out its root tea!

Just so we are on the same chaotic page:

Captain Aris just found out she has a long-lost sister. Beautiful, brutal, morally tangled Tavarin. And just when we thought we might get a heartwarming reunion? BOOM. Enter General Talos, looking like a villain handcrafted in a forge of nightmares, complete with a snake helmet, void-cane, and a ring that can turn your blood into a gravitational implosion. I mean, who gives a warlord a ring that powerful? That's style and terror all wrapped into one disturbing fashion statement.

Tavarin's end wasn't deserved right? Not to us. To me, it looked like someone trying to change, to love, to connect. And maybe that's what made it so tragic. She chose heart over orders. And we all saw what that cost her. And let's not ignore our fearless Captain. She stood her ground. Didn't flinch, didn't beg, just watched as someone who could've been her, if she'd made different choices, died before her. Maybe there could've been something between them. Some kind of reconnection. Now? That door's closed for good.

The crew's quiet now, maybe not fully because of Tavarin but because we've seen where this road leads if we don't stop it. Vengeance has a sound. And I'm betting we're about to hear it.

Anyway, I should get back to my nap in the Garden. It's not easy balancing cosmic commentary and hammock rotations.

**Broadcasting from beyond the blaze,**

Yours in mischief,

—Pixo

# Chapter 16

## SHACKLES AND SHADOWS

The volcanic winds had barely cooled before the cuffs clicked into place. Aris didn't resist, something deep had gone quiet inside her. Tavarin's death wasn't just an execution. It was a rupture, something sharp and sudden that left Aris hollow in places she hadn't realized were vulnerable.

She'd heard those last words, *"I'm sorry."* Too late to change anything. Too late to understand what Tavarin meant. Now they chased her through every heartbeat, tangled with questions that would never get answers. A sister revealed. A connection severed before it had time to take shape. Not grief, not exactly. Something quieter. Something colder. Regret, maybe. Or the ache of a door closing before she'd even decided to step through.

They marched Aris and the crew past the fractured gates of the volcanic castle, its obsidian towers still steaming with residual heat. Ash clung to every fold of her suit, falling from her like snowflakes. Behind her, she sensed her crew being stripped of their gear: Ralik's visor torn away, Thorne's gauntlets pried off with force, Fen restrained by cold wrists bound behind his back. None of them resisted. They had survived the Trial, but Talos had taken everything from them but their ship. If he wanted them dead, they already would be. He wanted something from them...answers, leverage, control. Whatever it was, it kept them breathing. For now.

Before them loomed a shadow greater than the castle itself, the ship Talos arrived in. An obsidian warship embedded into the mountain's side like a splinter driven into flesh. **The Graven.** Its name was stenciled across the hull, low and deliberate, carved as if the metal itself had groaned during its branding. The vessel consumed the surrounding light, its form swallowing even the mountain's glow. No engines thrummed. No beacons blinked. It was not a ship currently. It was something more. A sarcophagus wedged into the earth, waiting for the dead to rise.

As they approached, the boarding ramp extended with slow precision, metal settling into place like it had been waiting for them.

Aris felt the atmosphere thicken, not with heat, but with a pressure that made her chest clench. It wasn't gravity. It was the weight of something watching, something ancient. The Graven didn't welcome. It devoured.

Inside, the corridors stretched endlessly, illuminated only by dim red pulses embedded in the floor like coals beneath glass. The walls bore no insignias, no panels, no orientation, just seamless black surfaces, scored faintly as if the ship itself had once bled. Even their footsteps seemed muffled by the dry metallic air.

Guards peeled away her armor, taking with it the faint glow of the Root shard embedded during the trial. They shoved her into a chamber and sealed the door with a finality that caught in her throat. It wasn't loud. It was soft. Almost gentle. Like the closing of a tomb.

Her cell was neither spartan nor grotesque. It bore the hallmarks of deliberate control, a space too clean to be humane, too engineered to be ignored. The walls were smooth and unblemished, the corners rounded with surgical precision, and the soft overhead light cast no shadows, as if even darkness had been sterilized. It was not a cell meant to punish with pain or filth, it was meant to erase. Erase time, emotion, and memory. It offered nothing, not even resistance. Only silence.

Aris didn't sit on the cot. She took the floor instead, cross-legged, arms draped over her knees. Her eyes remained open, unblinking.

Tavarin's face came back to her, but not as a soldier. Not as a rival. Just a woman, pleading not for forgiveness, but for a future. For family. And Aris had stood there, surrounded, outnumbered, already too late. There hadn't been a choice. Not really. But still, she carried the weight of that moment like a splinter beneath her skin.

The guilt wasn't clean. It was jagged, pulling her from within. She'd faced war. Lost friends. Made decisions that cost lives. But this...this was different. Tavarin wasn't an enemy lost. She was a future unlived.

Aris exhaled slowly and forced her thoughts to shift. Thorne. Ralik. Fen. Pixo. She pictured them, not as soldiers, but as fragments of something fragile and real. Thorne's steady presence, his support deeper than most men's words. Ralik's mind, sharp as ever, always at war with his own emotions. Fen, with laughter that softened grief, courage wrapped in kindness. And then Pixo...gone, but never silent. She thought about what he would say in this situation.

*"Hey, Captain Hotface...cheer up. It's only a floating nightmare full of psychopaths. What could possibly go wrong?"*

Aris closed her eyes, letting a half-smile twitch at her lips. Just a flicker. Just enough.

Then she opened them again and looked around, not as a prisoner, but as a captain. Not for escape routes, not yet, but for patterns. Imperfections. A pulse in the wall that flickered a breath too slowly. A seam that vibrated slightly under pressure. Every structure had its flaw. She just had to find one here.

Because she would not break. She wouldn't stand idly by and allow the Olyssians to destroy another planet. And The Graven, for all its emptiness, had no idea what it had just swallowed whole.

Two days. That's how long they'd been stuck here, marched from cell to hall, from hall to cell, with no word from Command and no sign of their ship.

The dining hall reeked of control. Every element of the space was deliberate, from the metal tables bolted down like anchors to the mismatched chairs damaged by years of tension. The stench of overcooked meals seeped into the walls, barely masked by the harsh tang of antiseptic that lingered in the recycled air. Overhead, industrial lights hummed relentlessly, flooding the room with a clinical glare that flattened every expression and denied even the comfort of shadow. It wasn't just a dining hall, it was a stage where subjugation was ritualized three times a day. A silent sermon in concrete and steel.

Aris was ushered through the main entrance beneath the cold stare of black-armored guards, their presence more shadow than soldier. Her boots struck the metal flooring with a sharp rhythm that echoed louder than expected, drawing glances from nearby inmates. But she paid them no mind. Her eyes moved with purpose, scanning until they landed on a familiar group in the far corner, her crew. They were worn down but intact, Ralik noticed her first. His gaze lifted slowly, disbelieving, before his back straightened with quiet urgency. Fen followed, his shoulders slumping with visible relief.

"Captain?" Fen's voice cut softly across the sterile air, like a secret spoken aloud. He made to stand but hesitated, catching sight of the red-lensed camera eye in the wall. "You look like hell. Never been happier to see someone so thoroughly wrecked."

Aris offered a half-smile, her relief masked from habit. She slid into the seat across from them with a calm that felt more like muscle memory than serenity. "Nice to know your sense of timing and tact survived the internment."

Thorne didn't answer immediately. His nod was slow, deliberate, like his thoughts had weight he wasn't ready to share. "We heard you were in solitary confinement. We didn't know if we'd see you again. Time runs long in this place."

"They want it to," Aris replied. She took a moment to meet each of their eyes. Ralik's quiet sharpness, Fen's wary warmth, Thorne's ever-stalwart calm. "But we're here together now. That's what matters."

Ralik leaned in, voice low." It's not the guards. It's the air. This place is designed to dissolve you. Not all at once. It's erosion. They wear you down molecule by molecule."

Aris clasped her hands together on the table, her posture poised, eyes fierce. "Then we need to escape quickly. Until we can figure out a plan, we endure and hold each other together."

That was when the voice drifted over, dry and deliberate. "Hope's a strange flavor here. Bitter at first. But it lingers."

They turned to find an older man seated nearby, hunched over a gray tray. His skin looked like dried bark, sunken and weathered, his features half-swallowed by age and isolation. A milky film clouded one eye, but the other remained alert, studying them with quiet interest.

"Don't mind me," the man said, carving into his ration with eerie precision.

"My name's Keven. I've been here long enough to forget what the stars look like. I figured you were the ones Talos dragged in. We haven't seen new inmates in a long time. Most don't survive longer than a week."

Aris's voice was wary but level. "How have you survived this long?"

He didn't look up. "Most don't survive because they can't. This place breaks you down, but my kind...we're resistant to it due to our tough skin."

Thorne's jaw tightened, his gaze hard. "So, what's your angle, old man? You watching us for fun or are you trying to help us?"

Keven's laugh was low and weathered. "I have no angles. I've just been here long enough to know how this place operates, but I haven't been able to escape. Although I'm resistant, I've become weaker over time. I simply can't escape even if I tried."

Ralik shifted closer, suspicion and curiosity warring in his voice. "If you've got something to say, then say it. We don't have time for riddles."

He leaned closer, his voice quieting to a near hush. "The Graven thrives on conformity, on sameness. All the guards look the same, move the same, talk in code or not at all. They run like clockwork, shifts that never break pattern, uniforms that erase the man inside. I used to watch, thinking it was mindless. Now I know it's the only way to hide in plain sight."

He looked at Aris then, one brow raised. "You've got a crew with fight left in you. A strong arm, a clever mind, a brave soul, and someone crazy enough to lead them. You don't need a miracle. You need timing."

And with that, Keven stood and shuffled off, leaving behind his empty tray and something far more dangerous. Hope.

"Find out more information from him," Aris said looking at Fen.

"I'm on it, Captain." Fen replied.

"Ralik, start analyzing this place for weaknesses." Aris instructed.

"Of course," Ralik answered.

She rose to her feet, scanning each of them in turn. "And everyone...don't let this place break you. Survive. No matter what."

The showers were located at the far end of the prison block, beyond a set of magnetically sealed gates that released with a shrill buzz when authorized. The guard escorting Aris didn't speak, just motioned with a tilt of the head toward the steamy corridor ahead. She walked without resistance, her muscles aching from weeks of tension, her thoughts still weighted with the slow-burning pressure of Pixo's death and the crew's uncertain future.

The hallway leading to the coed showers was lined with slick obsidian tile, its black surface reflecting distorted shapes in the low red emergency lighting. The ever-present hum of the Graven's systems vibrated faintly underfoot, like a dormant heartbeat beneath steel skin. The heat in the corridor rose with every step. Moisture clung to the air, thickening around her skin. By the time she reached the entrance, the world outside the fogged threshold had already started to blur.

She stepped inside. Steam billowed like ghostly veils, curling around the half-visible forms of other prisoners already washing away the grime of another day. The sound of rushing water masked soft conversation, and the occasional bark of guards posted just outside. Aris moved toward an unoccupied stall at the far end, unfastening the coarse inmate uniform at the collar. She let it slip from her shoulders and fall to the floor, leaving her bare beneath the lights and steam.

She stood there for a moment, letting the hot stream cascade down her back. The sting of heat against her skin was welcome. It reminded her she was still alive, still here. Her mind wandered, toward Ralik's quiet steadiness, the way he'd watched her without judgment. And then toward Thorne, always a presence beside her, immovable, his strength a silent promise.

The sound of footsteps behind her pulled her from her thoughts. Thorne entered first, his massive frame briefly silhouetted through the fog, muscles tensed from days without rest. He didn't speak, but his eyes met hers. They were soft for just a heartbeat before he turned to take the stall across from her. This was the first time they'd truly seen each other stripped of everything. And maybe, for the first time, she wanted that. Wanted to be seen by him, by Ralik. She felt closer to them now, the walls she'd built around herself quietly unraveling, thread by thread.

Water poured over him, and she caught herself watching the way it moved down the ridges of his chest, over his abdomen and lower. He was built like a fortress, and part of her hated how safe that made her feel, because needing anyone felt like weakness she couldn't afford. He glanced sideways only once more, eyes flicking toward her as if caught between instinct and restraint.

Then Ralik followed. He was leaner, quieter in his movements, his presence a sharp contrast to Thorne's grounded mass. But his form surprised her, it was more athletic than she imagined, his stomach marked with defined muscle and taut skin, his posture modest but unhidden. He hesitated at the threshold, eyes scanning for a stall until he saw Aris. For a moment, his breath visibly caught.

She didn't flinch under his gaze. Neither did she hide. Instead, she stepped into the water more fully, letting the water run down her face and chest, over the full curve of her hips, her thighs slick with heat and mist. She ran her hands across her body with a bar of soap. Gently caressing the day's dirt away.

Her gaze dipped for only a breath, catching the fullness of Thorne and Ralik in the fog. It wasn't lewd, it was involuntary, curious, a startled awareness of the quiet confidence each man carried even now. Thorne's was unsurprising, matching the rest of him, unapologetically formidable. Ralik's, though less imposing, carried a massive grace, a symmetry that made her chest tighten unexpectedly. She wasn't supposed to notice. But she did. And for once, she let herself feel attraction.

The tension between the three of them simmered there in the mist, unspoken but undeniable. Thorne scrubbed his hands through his hair, pretending not to watch, but his eyes drifted again. Ralik adjusted the shower's pressure, but his gaze lingered just a moment too long.

Aris caught them both, and a small, unreadable smile touched the corner of her lips. She felt it too. The questions neither of them had dared to ask, the tether pulled tight between strength, intellect, and desire.

Ralik and Thorne glanced at each other for a moment, their excitement unmistakable. There was an acknowledgment between them, brief but charged.

She turned her back and continued rinsing, giving them space while her heart raced loudly beneath her ribs. The heat was no longer just from the steam. Something had shifted between the three of them. It was undeniable, their powerful connection.

# Chapter 17

## ESCAPE FROM THE ENGRAVED

T he cold metal of her cot pressed against Aris's back, but it wasn't discomfort that kept her awake. She lay still, eyes fixed on the low ceiling of her cell, watching shadows shift with the pulse of the red emergency lights that throbbed through the corridors of the Graven. Her skin still carried the memory of steam and silence, of the shower mist clinging to her like a second skin long after she had returned to confinement. It wasn't just warmth she remembered, it was the way their glances lingered, the way her breath had caught at the raw humanity of it all. That moment had stripped them down further than the prison ever could.

It wasn't lust, at least not entirely. It was clarity. In the haze of routine and oppression, something primal had stirred, not just in her, but in them all. A pulse of life beneath the chokehold of Talos's dominion.

When the cell door slid open with its usual hiss, Aris didn't move right away. She sat up slowly, spine straight, eyes sharper than they had been in days. Her body ached less now from the rough bed. There was a grit in her breath, a rhythm returning to her bones.

The dining hall buzzed with a faint mechanical hum, the overhead lights casting long, sterile shadows across the floor. At the far end of the hall, a narrow catwalk spanned the upper level, a skeletal platform of grated steel suspended beneath thick support beams. Armed guards paced there in slow, methodical circuits, their rifles slung casually but within easy reach. From this elevated perch, they had an unbroken view of the inmates below, a constant reminder of who held control. Harsh floodlights ringed the catwalk, casting down stark cones of illumination that bled across the mess of tables and prisoners.

The crew gathered at a table near the edge of the guard's line of sight, shoulders hunched but eyes alert. They didn't speak for a while, each of them stirring at their bland rations. Thorne's jaw worked with barely checked tension. Ralik's fingers drummed quiet patterns, his gaze sweeping the ceiling, tracing unseen lines. Fen offered a half-smile, faint but genuine. When Aris arrived, she didn't sit, she stood behind her chair, palms flat on the cold surface of the table.

"It's time for us to break out of here," Aris said quietly. Her voice didn't tremble, though the weight behind it pressed into the stillness between them like gravity. "We need to finish the escape plan."

Thorne leaned forward, arms folded tight. "What do we need to do?"

"Ralik was able to find a weakness in the guards patrol pattern," she replied.

Ralik looked up, his eyes meeting Aris's. "Yes," he said, voice quiet but clear. "I found only one inconsistency."

Thorne drummed his fingers against the table, a restless edge in his movements. "Then let's stop wasting time. What do we need to pull this off?"

Ralik tapped his fingers against the edge of the table, eyes scanning the room as if visualizing the entire layout of the prison. "I've noticed one of them is slower than the rest, probably nursing an old injury. He's our best shot. We need to get him alone and take him out quietly. We can use his uniform to escape. "

Aris's expression sharpened. "Once we have the uniform, we need someone who can sell it. Fen, you confident?"

Fen gave a slow nod, his usual brightness dimmed by the weight of what they were planning. "I've been watching how they move. It's stiff, robotic almost with no eye contact, no conversation. I can match that. I'll need a keycard, though."

Ralik nodded. "That's part of the risk. Once you have the uniform on, you'll lead us in cuffs. That's how we can blend into their system."

Thorne grunted. "And if they call for a ID verification on the keycard?"

"We act," Aris said, voice steady. "We stay in character, but if it turns sideways, we improvise. We've survived worse than suspicion."

Thorne's eyes scanned the area, jaw tight. "We're not making it far without our gear."

"We won't," Aris said, voice steady. "We'll get it back."

Ralik shifted, mind already working. "The armory's likely midship. Restricted access. Monitored corridors."

Fen kept his head low, voice hushed. "Uniforms would make things easier. I passed a laundry access corridor on the way to the mess, not far from the last checkpoint."

Aris nodded. "Then we need to get a fresh set for everyone. Fen, it's all up to you to lead us."

"I'm on it, Captain!" Fen replied. The timing had to be perfect.

Later that day, the mess hall was noisy but tense, its low hum of conversation always a breath away from eruption. Aris sat across from Ralik, their meal trays barely touched. She gave a slight nod. That was the signal.

Ralik stood first, slow and deliberate. Then he tipped his tray hard across the table, slamming it into Aris's chest. The clatter of utensils and synthetic slop hitting the floor echoed like a shot.

Aris shot to her feet, eyes wide with fury. "You want to try that again?" she barked, loud enough to turn heads.

Ralik shoved her shoulder. "You don't give orders anymore, Captain."

Guards on the catwalk looked up. Others stepped in from the walls, voices raised. "Back to your seats!"

Aris lunged, tackling Ralik to the ground. The room exploded in chaos. Boots slamming against metal, inmates laughing and yelling as the scuffle ignited a chain reaction. Two more prisoners jumped in for the fun of it. The guards rushed in to break it up.

But in the shadows of that commotion, Fen and Thorne slipped out the side exit, quiet as ghosts. They moved down the auxiliary corridor, pace quick but measured. The infirmary wing had no cameras, maybe from being too old, too forgotten, or just left broken long ago. This wing was sparsely patrolled, and the soft clink of armor on the tile ahead signaled their target was near. They'd watched this guard's routine for days. Always passing through during the dining block, always alone, always slow. They saw him favoring his right leg, baton clipped lazily at his side. He didn't even notice their approach.

Thorne lunged first, wrapping one massive arm around the guard's throat and lifting him off his feet before he could cry out. Fen caught the man's arms, helping to pull him backward into the darkened maintenance corridor.

It was over in seconds. The guard sunk unconscious, wedged against a crate. Fen worked fast, unbuckling the armor and slipping into the black uniform. It was a tight fit, but close enough. He snapped on the helmet and retrieved the keycard and cuffs.

Thorne glanced back toward the distant din of shouting. "Think they'll hold the attention long enough?"

"They will," Fen said, voice distorted behind the visor. "We've got a window. Let's move."

The mess hall was still a storm of chaos when Fen strode in, helmet secured, posture rigid. To anyone watching, he looked like any other Olyssian enforcer clad in black armor. He was faceless, emotionless, another cog in the black machine. He moved with purpose, navigating the fray like it was routine.

He dragged Thorne beside him in cuffs, the larger man slouched and scowling as if mid-punishment.

Fen walked up to a couple of officers who were placing Ralik and Aris in handcuffs.

"Transfer order just came through," Fen said through the helmet's comm-distorted voice, crisp and authoritative. "Unit D-9. These three are flagged for behavioral review by General Talos."

One of the guards narrowed his eyes beneath his visor. "These two just started a riot. Protocol says we send them to lower holding first."

Fen didn't hesitate. "Override. Direct processing. Talos wants them looked at together as part of an aggression chain. Delay, and it's your name on the report."

The guard cursed under his breath, clearly weighing the risk of going against what looked like an official order. Around them, more officers were still separating inmates and barking commands. Every second spent arguing was another problem.

"Fine. They're yours. Take the trash out."

The cuffs on Aris and Ralik clicked into place, and they were pushed toward Fen. He caught Aris by the arm, firm but not rough.

With the three "prisoners" in tow, Fen turned them toward the exit. Their steps fell into a practiced rhythm, their breathing synced to nerves and precision. Every corridor they passed felt like a test of balance between urgency and normalcy, between concealment and collapse.

They said nothing until they rounded the first blind corner. "Where to?" Thorne muttered under his breath, barely moving his lips.

"Uniforms," Aris said quietly. "First priority. Then the armory."

"We need to get to the laundry room," Fen replied. "Keven said he used to work a detail in the laundry room. It's on the second floor."

They moved as shadows, each step carefully placed. One wrong turn and it would all fall apart.

But so far, the rhythm held. And just ahead, they reached the ship's elevator. They entered, Fen hit the second floor after scanning his newly acquired keycard.

The elevator doors slid closed with a quiet hiss, muffling the chaos of the mess hall behind them.

Inside, the quiet was louder. The hum of the lift filled the space between their quickened heartbeats.

Ralik shifted slightly in his cuffs, his voice barely audible. "You think the uniforms will still be in rotation storage?"

"They have to be," Fen replied, eyes fixed on the floor count slowly ticking upward. "Keven said laundry detail handles distribution for night shift around this time."

Thorne rolled his shoulders, the cuffs creaking against his bulk. "If there's anyone in there?"

"We overpower them," Aris said. Her voice was calm, but beneath it ran steel. "No killing unless it's the only option."

The elevator dinged as the doors opened. They stepped out into a quieter corridor, narrower and less patrolled than the ones below. The overhead lights buzzed faintly, flickering once as they turned the corner toward a small access door marked with a faded stencil: *UNIFORM SERVICES – BAY 02B.*

At the panel by the door, Fen tapped the stolen keycard, tension straining in his neck as he waited for the scan. A brief second passed. Then the light blinked green. The locking mechanism clicked open.

Inside, rows of Olyssian uniforms hung in military order, the metallic scent of synthetic fibers and recycled detergent heavy in the air. A single ventilation duct whirred in the upper corner, masking the sound of their steps as they moved quickly between racks.

"Move fast," Fen muttered, already pulling down suits in their approximate sizes.

Ralik was the first to shed his prison top, his movements swift and meticulous. He snatched a uniform with the insignia matching Fen's and began dressing. Thorne pulled on his gear next, his sheer size making the process less graceful but just as urgent. He reached for a bag and slung it over his shoulder.

Aris stripped without hesitation, her back straight, expression unreadable as she donned the black undersuit. Her skin stood in contrast to the pristine lining of the Olyssian gear. The uniform molded to her curves perfectly. She moved with quiet precision, each motion controlled, as if the uniform weren't a disguise at all but something familiar.

Ralik stole a glance her way, a flicker of awe quickly buried beneath focus. He finished making last adjustments to his uniform.

Once suited, the four of them looked like any other Olyssian squad: cold, masked, anonymous.

"The armory's next," Ralik said, quickly moving toward the exit.

"Keven said it was two wings over, middle deck," Fen added. "Probably coded entry and monitored. We walk fast, stay quiet, and don't give anyone a reason to stop us."

"Let's move!" Aris said, as they walked toward the door.

Fen adjusted his gloves, tucking the keycard into a compartment on his hip. "We're on delivery detail. That's the lie. If anyone asks, it's a sweep for Talos."

They stepped out into the hallway again, formation natural. They walked shoulder-to-shoulder, almost in step with each other. Whatever waited beyond the next corridor, they were ready to meet it together. And the armory, the final test of the night, loomed just ahead.

The corridor to the armory narrowed with each step, the crew moving quickly now. Clad in stolen Olyssian uniforms, they projected confidence, but each heartbeat ticked like a countdown. Fen led the group with calculated authority, helmet secured, posture rigid. Behind him, Aris walked with her chin lifted, her eyes sharp beneath her visor. Ralik and Thorne followed in perfect step, carrying the weight of improvised purpose.

The final checkpoint loomed just ahead, an entry control station guarded by a single officer stationed beside the heavy blast doors of the armory. A biometric scanner and keypad blinked dimly in standby. The guard noticed their approach and straightened, placing a gloved hand over his belt as his gaze swept over them.

"Hold it there," he called, voice filtered through his helmet. "Authorization?"

Fen stepped forward without hesitation and slid the stolen keycard through the reader. A beep acknowledged the attempt, but instead of unlocking the door, a small display flashed red and brought up a holographic ID photo. It wasn't his face.

The guard frowned beneath his visor, his stance shifting slightly into alertness. "That doesn't look like you," he said flatly, his hand inching closer to his sidearm. The air between them grew taut, an invisible wire ready to snap.

Fen tensed for a split second, but Aris was already stepping forward, a breath ahead of trouble. She unclasped her helmet, letting it swing casually from her fingertips, and tilted her head just slightly, her expression switching from soldier to something far more disarming. "That's because he's filling in for Corporal John, poor guy twisted his knee during drills yesterday," she said, her voice smooth, a hint of mischief in her tone.

The guard blinked, clearly thrown off by her confidence and the sudden presence of curves not usually found among Olyssian ranks.

"You're sharp," Aris continued, stepping a little closer, her voice dropping just enough to invite rather than challenge. "And so handsome. Bet they're already talking about moving you up the chain."

The guard's mouth twitched in what might have been the beginning of a smile. "Well, I...uh, just doing my job."

She leaned in, just close enough for her voice to lower conspiratorially. "You're doing it damn well. Tell you what, once we're back from this little escort run, how about I let you buy me dinner? Tomorrow night. I hear the dining galley has a breathtaking steak dinner when they're trying to impress."

He blinked again, this time completely stunned, eyes darting between her and the crew behind her. "Wait...you're serious?"

Aris let her smile soften, her tone dipped just slightly into teasing. "I wouldn't offer if I wasn't. You strike me as someone who'd know how to enjoy the moment."

The guard hesitated one more second, then shook his head with a chuckle, a slight flush creeping into his face. "Alright, go on. Just don't make me regret it."

"You won't," she said with a wink.

He keyed in his credentials, and the heavy blast doors parted with a hiss, opening into the dimly lit vault of the armory.

As they stepped through, Aris exhaled slowly and replaced her helmet. Thorne gave a low whistle once they were out of earshot.

"You scare me more than the guns in here," he muttered.

"I take that as a compliment," she replied smoothly.

Ralik smirked and opened the inventory panel. "Locker 9-F. Third row down."

Thorne strode ahead and yanked it open, revealing their gear. Each piece was exactly the way it was before. Their weapons. Their armor. Their identities.

Aris ran her hand along her blasters before tossing it in the bag that Thorne had held on his shoulder. They all ensured their armor and weapons were fit snugly in the bag.

Thorne hefted the bag across his back, its weight solid and reassuring. Ralik gave one final glance toward the vault controls to confirm nothing had triggered. "No alerts," he said under his breath. "We're ghosts on their logs, for now."

"Then let's not linger," Aris murmured.

They exited the armory in formation, drawing no unwanted attention to themselves. Even the armory guard gave them a quick smile as they left.

The front access corridor stretched before them like a clean, clinical promise. It was the brightest part of the ship, wide and sterile, with high-gloss floors reflecting the floodlights overhead. Along the walls, security terminals blinked softly, monitored by guards stationed like statues at each checkpoint. It was a place designed for control, for final inspection. And now, it was their path to freedom.

Fen led the group, posture straight, movements clipped and confident. Thorne carried the heavy gear bag slung over his shoulder with ease, like it was just another assignment loadout. Ralik walked in harmony. Aris moved like she had worn this armor her whole life, head high, stride commanding, a superior beneath the skin of the enemy.

As they approached the final checkpoint, the last two guards turned toward them. Their faces were hidden behind mirrored visors, but their rifles were at rest, slung diagonally across their chests, not yet raised. One of them stepped forward, scanning the group with routine boredom.

"Unit tag?" the guard asked, gesturing lazily toward Fen.

Fen held out the keycard they'd stolen, tapping it against the terminal without a word. The soft beep of authorization echoed louder than it should have in the pause.

The guard's visor turned slightly toward Thorne's bag. "Heavy load. Gear transfer?"

Aris stepped forward smoothly, her tone clipped but professional. She knew the jargon well enough to sell it, Olyssian bureaucracy never changed. "Reassignment from upper-level confiscation to ground command. Direct order. The logs are already synced to main."

There was a pause. Just long enough to feel dangerous. Then the guard gave a short nod. "Proceed."

The outer hatch hissed, hydraulics whining as the massive doors unlocked. A wash of hot, volcanic air filled the corridor, thick with soot and the faint tang of scorched minerals. The outside world flooded in, not safe, but wide open.

They stepped through together. Boots met dirt. Red-tinged soil crunched beneath their feet. The haze of the ash-heavy atmosphere made the sun look like a bleeding eye behind clouds. But they didn't stop to admire it.

Behind them, the blast doors sealed shut again with a final thud, cold metal separating the past from the present.

They kept walking, their gear hidden in plain sight, their expressions unreadable beneath enemy visors. No alarms sounded. No one called them back. The crew of the *Zephira Dawn* didn't run. They didn't look back. They walked into the scorched wasteland with the posture of soldiers and the souls of survivors.

Joseph Young

And though the armor on their backs wasn't theirs,
the fire in their chests was unmistakable. They weren't
just free. They were in motion. And they were heading
straight for the castle, where General Talos waited.
They were running out of time to stop him.

# Chapter 18

## PIXO S POSTSCRIPT #4

Coming to you live from my beanbag chair that's made of the softest clouds.

Whew! Okay, reader, take a *deep breath*. Because that was wild.

I mean seriously, they just spent days locked inside the darkest, most brutal prison in recorded history. The Graven! A place so bleak, it makes a black hole look like a vacation spot. And what did they do? Oh, you know, just pulled off the boldest prison break since someone said, "what if we just *walked out*?"

And somehow, they made it look good. Real good. But before we go any further, you might wanna pause and grab some water. Hydrate. Because let's be honest, you're probably still overheating from that *shower scene*. Don't lie, I saw you gripping the page a little tighter. Steam was jumping off the words like they were written on lava rock. Aris. Thorne. Ralik. All in the same room. All wet. All *very* not ignoring each other.

Whew!

Honestly, I didn't know whether to blush or cheer. Or both.

But as wild as it got in there, things are only heating up. Because now they're out...and headed straight for the volcanic Castle. Yeah, *that* place. The one looming on the horizon like a bad omen in armor.

And guess who's still waiting for them?

General Talos. Big, angry, and probably in desperate need of a hobby that doesn't involve war crimes.

I'm worried about them. I mean, I know they've got grit, guts, and matching trauma scars but Talos isn't just another checkpoint guard. He's the end-of-level boss that makes you throw your controller across the room after losing to him over and over again.

So, take a sip, stretch your neck, and maybe say a little wish to the stars.

Because this crew? They're not just escaping anymore.

They're heading into the fire.

—Pixo

# Chapter 19

## CASTLE OF CRIMSON COMMAND

Volcanic haze clung to the sky like bruised fire, streaking the clouds in shades of copper and blood. Beneath a jagged rock ledge just south of the fortress, the crew of the *Zephira Dawn* crouched low in silence. The Castle loomed ahead with black stone walls veined with molten heat. It pulsed like a living wound carved into the mountainside, a fortress born from fury.

Ralik tapped quickly on his datapad, syncing their latest findings to a secure uplink. Within moments, Command's response crackled through their comms, sharp and clear.

"Confirmed intel on General Talos' involvement changes your directive," came Admiral Veyra's clipped tone through the line. "You are authorized to engage. Prevent further planetary compromise by any means necessary."

Aris exchanged a look with her crew, no hesitation now. Orders were orders, but this time, they aligned with purpose.

"Reinforcements are enroute," Veyra continued. "ETA, one cycle. You won't have to hold the line alone for long."

Ralik locked the datapad away. "One day until backup arrives. Until then, it's just us."

Thorne dropped the heavy duffel on the dirt beside them. "Time to suit up properly," he said, rolling his shoulder. "This bag's been whining for attention."

One by one, they peeled off their Olyssian disguises, each snap of a clasp and tug of a sleeve like shedding a lie. Inside the bag, their original gear waited: armor worn from battle and heat-hardened, weapons tuned to their touch, tech enhancements still buzzing with Guardian-gifted energy. Aris slid into her armor with slow reverence. This time, it glowed faintly, pulsing with power beneath the surface.

Ralik locked his visor into place, running a systems check. "Power levels are elevated. Guardian energy's still syncing with our gear."

Fen double-checked the chamber on his rifle and cocked it with a grin. "Then let's give these Olyssians a lightshow they'll never forget."

They surveyed the gate below. Steel reinforcements. Twin towers. Interlocking patrol routes. No weakness, no gap, no leniency.

Thorne let out a grunt. "The castle is swarming with Olyssian guards. How do we get through?"

"Straight through the front gate," Aris replied with a hint of resolve.

They moved like a stormfront, each one ready, synced in rhythm without a word more. Aris stepped forward, planting her boots into the blackened soil. With a twist of her wrists, her twin blasters charged up, arcs of plasma crawling across the metal casings like lightning itching to be set free.

A distant horn blew from the battlements above. Olyssian troops began to cluster at the top of the towers, rifles ready. But they were too late.

"Light it up," Aris said.

Fen raised his rifle, its core glowing. With a single blast, the front gate erupted into a column of shrapnel and flame. The earth shook as molten rock scattered across the courtyard. The gate had not opened, it had been annihilated.

Through the smoke, they charged. Thorne led the assault, shoulder-slamming the first enemy who staggered forward, sending the armored guard flying into a wall with a crack loud enough to echo. Before the next could react, Fen's rifle barked, a high-pitched pulse snapping into the guard's chestplate, sending sparks into the air.

Aris ducked under a swing of a plasma halberd, rolled to the side, and came up blasting, twin bolts slamming into the legs of two advancing Olyssians, knocking them to the scorched ground. Her shots weren't just weapons anymore; they were extensions of her fury, her survival, her strong will.

Ralik moved like a whisper through the storm of combat, visor glowing faintly with rapid pulses of Guardian energy. Streams of translucent data scrolled across his lens, mapping every heat source, weapon charge, and micro-movement around him. As one of the larger Olyssian brutes lunged toward Thorne from the flank, Ralik's eyes narrowed.

"Left side, three seconds!" he shouted.

Ralik pivoted before the brute even reached full stride, sliding a shock disc across the floor. It skidded precisely into place, just as the guard's boot hit metal. A surge of electric current jolted up through the soldier's armor, locking his limbs mid-stride.

"Now!" Ralik barked.

Thorne didn't hesitate. He spun and drove a gauntleted fist square into the brute's chest, the impact denting the black alloy like crumpled tin and sending the man crashing into the stone wall behind him.

Ralik was already moving again, ghosting between skirmishes, calling out threats a heartbeat before they materialized. With every shift in enemy stance, every flicker of a weapon charge, his scanner whispered secrets the Olyssians didn't know they were giving away. And with those secrets, the crew danced one step ahead of death.

More guards swarmed the courtyard, dozens at a time, but the crew didn't slow.

An Olyssian sniper caught sight of Fen and fired, a searing beam grazed his shoulder, but his armor absorbed the impact with only a ripple of energy distortion. He winced, but it didn't stop him.

"Is that all you've got?" he muttered through clenched teeth, aiming his rifle and returning fire. The shot cracked through the air, striking the sniper's perch and sending the soldier tumbling down in a blaze of sparks and flame.

Another wave came through the side corridor with five soldiers armed with rifles and riot shields. Ralik shouted, "Right flank!"

Aris turned on instinct, powered up her left blaster, and fired a concussive burst that knocked the front two off their feet. Thorne rushed the gap, roaring as he brought his fists down on one of the guards, then used the shield like a battering ram to smash into the rest.

The power flowing through them was undeniable. Shots rang out, blades clashed, smoke curled through the air, and still, they pressed forward. Even when they took hits, burns, bruises, near-misses, their armor held. Not because it was perfect, but because it had been infused with the Guardian's shard.

Ralik paused behind a statue of molten stone, panting, visor cracked at the edge. "We're cutting through them faster than they can regroup. This is our moment."

Thorne chuckled, blood on his gauntlets. "Feels good to hit harder than them for once."

They regrouped at the base of the central courtyard steps, their boots crunching over shattered stone and broken helmets. Around them, the courtyard lay quiet now, except for the hiss of molten rock and the dying crackle of sparking rifles. Piles of defeated Olyssians were strewn in every direction, their once-disciplined ranks crumpled beneath the fury of the Zephira Dawn crew. Aris stood tall, shoulders squared, scanning the battlefield they'd carved. Her crew surrounded her, breathing hard, but still standing. Still burning with iron will.

Ahead, the steps rose in a grand spiral, wide and unyielding, curling into the jagged opening at the volcano's throat. A throne gate loomed above them, an obsidian archway glowing with heat, its silhouette writhing in the flickering light. Somewhere beyond those walls, General Talos pursued the heart of Pyronyx.

Behind them, the heavy gate they'd stormed through still smoked, twisted steel and shattered defenses marking their arrival with violent precision. Smoke drifted upward like a war banner raised in defiance.

Above, the skies deepened into a sickly, blood-red hue. The light bent strangely now, casting elongated shadows that flickered like ghosts across the volcanic stone. The mountain let out a low moan, ancient and primal. A tremor passed beneath their feet, shaking loose pebbles from the cliffside. Cracks formed at the peak of the volcano, glowing red from within. Lava began to pour in slow rivulets down its flanks, carving glowing veins into the black rock like the castle itself was bleeding.

The fortress was fused to the mountain, its spires jutting from the lower cliffs while much of its mass tunneled deep into the volcanic rock. The steps they followed wound upward along the inner wall, carved from cooled magma and scorched stone, leading them deeper into the mountain's heart.

A tremor rolled beneath them like a living thing, snarling through the earth with bone-deep resonance. Dust scattered in plumes as chunks of rock dislodged from above and crashed against the obsidian ramparts. The crew turned instinctively, eyes locking on the volcano's crown.

Molten light pulsed through the fresh cracks like veins in an open wound. The slow spill of lava turned to a steady flow, oozing down the flanks in multiple streams. Each glowing path illuminated the fortress in flickering gold and crimson, making it look less like a castle and more like a demon's throne hewn from the planet's core.

Aris's jaw clenched as she steadied her footing. "The volcano is beginning to erupt! He must be getting close."

"Yes," Ralik murmured, visor reflecting the distant rivers of flame. "But we still have time."

A sudden blast echoed from the summit like the exhale of a buried giant. A geyser of ash burst upward in the distance, raining black cinders that danced in the swirling wind. The air thickened, hotter now, laced with smoke and sulfur that coated their tongues with bitterness.

They moved together through the wreckage, the aftershocks keeping time like a ticking clock. Lava veins twisted through the stone beneath them, lighting their path with unnatural radiance. The mountain groaned again, and a shower of molten pebbles arced from above, clattering harmlessly against their armor.

Fen looked up toward the smoking summit and exhaled. "We are going into the fire now."

"Yes," Aris said, tightening her grip on her blaster. "We need to stop Talos from getting that heart."

Behind them, the last of the guards smoldered in ruin. They had left the castle behind. Ahead, the path wound upward, into the heat, into the storm, into whatever wrath the mountain had yet to give. The fire was rising. And so were they.

# Chapter 20

## FIRESTORM FINALE

The heat thickened as they ascended, pressing against their lungs and curling along their skin like invisible tendrils of flame. Molten veins lined the castle walls, glowing brighter the deeper they ventured. Every step echoed with tension. The stone beneath their boots pulsed, as if the fortress itself were alive, angry, and aware.

Ralik's visor flickered with streams of data, his voice low but clear. "Energy spike ahead. It's not just heat...this is the Heart. The convergence point is close."

Aris wiped the sweat from her brow, her armor shimmering faintly under the Guardian-forged enhancements. "Everyone stay sharp. General Talos will be close."

Thorne gave a short grunt of agreement. His powered gauntlets flexed in anticipation, red energy humming just beneath the surface. "If he could've taken it by force already, he would have. The Heartspire must be resisting him. He's still looking for a way in or a way to control it."

Fen jogged beside them, rifle slung across his shoulder. Despite the tension in his jaw, his voice kept its usual grit of levity. "You ever think about how we always end up walking *toward* the glowing death room instead of away from it?"

"Every damn day," Ralik laughed.

The staircase gave way to a steep ramp, carved directly into the volcanic stone. Jagged spires jutted from the walls like broken teeth, and smoke hissed from hidden vents along the edges. The higher they climbed, the more the ground vibrated beneath their feet.
After walking for a couple of minutes, they reached the massive archway, its edges warped and half-melted from years of unforgiving heat. Beyond it stretched a cavernous magma chamber, the molten core of the volcano. It was like standing in the throat of a dragon, its breath hot and relentless.

Lava surged in wide, jagged rivers along channels carved into the obsidian floor. The air shimmered with rising heat, thick with ash and the distant rumble of tectonic pressure. Crimson light danced across the jagged ceiling, reflecting off mineral like lines of fire pulsing through the earth itself. Their armor systems worked overtime, cooling their cores and regulating their body temperature, shielding them just enough to keep moving through heat that would have melted bone.

At the very center of the chamber, suspended above a swirling basin of magma, hovered the second Planetary Heart...glowing, thrumming, angry. It radiated power like a second sun, drawing embers toward it in lazy, gravitational spirals.

And there, standing in front of it, was **General Talos.**

Talos stood tall atop a blackened dais, his obsidian cane now fully unsheathed. The blade shimmered unnaturally, edges pulsing like a wound in space itself. At his side, the gravity-forged ring on his hand flickered with silent menace.

He looked down at them like a judge already confident in his verdict. "So," Talos said, his voice echoing across the chamber like a funeral bell, "the broken crew limps to my door. Dressed like warriors but fraying at the seams."

Aris stepped forward, eyes burning. "You thought locking us away would stop us. You were wrong."

"Perhaps," he replied coldly. "You look tired, Captain. And yet...you're still leading them into the fire."

He gestured to the hovering Heart behind him, flames curling upward like hands reaching for a god.

"The guardian of this heart put up a good fight but now this is nearly mine. Just like the first, you're too late to stop what's coming."

Thorne stepped forward beside Aris, fists clenched at his sides." Watch us."

Talos cocked his head, the slightest smirk tugging at his lips. "Still hiding behind your muscle. And the clever one," he added, nodding toward Ralik. "I've read the reports. You predict patterns, yes? Let's see how well your scans fare when your bones are cracking."

Ralik's visor glowed faintly. "You're not as unreadable as you think."

"And you're not as immortal as you hope," Talos replied, raising his blade. There was no signal, only the shared breath before the storm.

Aris surged forward, dual pistols blazing radiant streaks through the smoky air. Talos deflected the first volley with his cane blade, void energy rippling outward in a pulse of unseen force. The blast caught her mid-stride and hurled her backward, boots skidding across cracked stone.

Thorne charged next, activating his power gauntlets mid-run. Crimson shields bloomed from his arms just in time to absorb Talos's retaliatory strike, a brutal downward swing that cracked the volcanic stone beneath their feet.

Fen circled to the right, rifle up, peppering Talos from the side. For a moment, it seemed the distraction worked, until the general raised his ring hand. A pulse of gravity erupted from him in a silent wave, knocking Fen off his feet and into a pile of scorched stone. His rifle skidded across the floor, glowing hot.

Ralik stayed back, his scanner buzzing wildly. His visor filtered the energy patterns around Talos, revealing micro-movements and power surges a second before they happened. "Aris! Left flank, he's winding up!"

She ducked under Talos's backswing just in time, firing an arc of glowing blasts into his side. The impact staggered him, but only for a second.

Talos roared, lifting his ring hand again, and a silent gravitational spike pulsed into Thorne's chest. The brute dropped to one knee, shield flaring red, but held the line.

"I feel...heavier," Thorne grunted through clenched teeth, his gauntlets straining under the weight.

Ralik dove forward, baton gripped tight. He ducked under a horizontal strike and swung low, slamming the weapon into Talos's side, redirecting the force just as his scanner had predicted. But Talos pivoted with alarming speed and drove an elbow into Ralik's chest, sending him tumbling.

"You're persistent," Talos growled, dragging his cane blade in a wide arc, slicing glowing symbols into the floor. Lava burst upward in columns, separating the team.

Aris rolled through the blast radius, panting, with smoke filling her lungs from the volcano's blasts. She could see her team struggling to keep up the assault. The Heart chamber pulsed with unnatural energy, the very air turning molten with heat. Their strike had been bold, timed with precision but Talos had barely flinched. His power clearly outmatched theirs.

"Keep pressing!" Aris shouted, her voice hoarse over the roar of fire and steel.

Thorne surged forward with his shield gauntlets raised, absorbing a blast of heated force hurled by Talos's gravity ring. The impact knocked him backward, boots skidding across the volcanic stone. He slammed his gauntlets into the ground, deploying a temporary energy barrier that shimmered with strain. "He's too strong!"

Aris circled wide, her dual pistols lighting up the gloom with a blaze of radiant bursts. She struck true, each round slamming into Talos's armor, but it barely slowed him. The plating hissed where the shots landed.

Fen flanked left, rolling into cover behind a pillar of cooled lava. He emerged in a burst of motion, rifle raised, squeezing off a series of controlled bursts. "Come on, come on," His shots struck the side of Talos's helm, making him stagger.

Talos turned toward Fen, eyes aglow with searing crimson. With a subtle twist of his ring, a surge of invisible force punched the air.

Fen was ripped from the ground mid-shot, slammed into the stone wall like a ragdoll. He dropped, dazed and bleeding, trying to crawl toward his weapon.

"Fen!" Ralik broke from cover, sprinting across the chamber. His scanner over one eye flickered with a stream of energy readouts. "He's rerouting his center of mass, watch his right!"

Aris moved, trusting the call. She ducked under Talos's arcing blade swing, firing into his side. But Talos adapted faster than before. With a smirk, he grabbed Aris by the collar and hurled her toward Thorne. She crashed into her teammate's shield, knocking both to the floor in a tangle of limbs and armor.

Ralik dashed for Fen, helping him to reach cover. His visor hummed with predictive overlays, revealing Talos's next strike before it came. He dodged a blast of gravity spikes, then ducked under a second swipe of the obsidian blade as he advanced. With timing guided by the scanner, he struck Talos with a short, sharp punch to the side, barely enough to stagger the giant.

Talos growled, his eyes narrowing on Ralik now. "Clever," he muttered, voice dripping with menace. "But not clever enough."

The general reached out, his cane blade retracted and clenched in one hand. The other hand extended, the ring shimmering with gravitational charge. Ralik's chest seized as a force like needles filled his bloodstream. He screamed, dropping to his knees, scanner sparking from overload.

"Ralik!" Aris rose again, blood in her mouth. She launched herself at Talos with her pistols glowing white-hot from overuse. She screamed as she fired, twin beams slamming into Talos's chestplate.

He staggered, smoke rising from his armor but then he smiled. "So predictable. But do you really think this is the extent of my power?"

He swung his cane blade in a wide arc, tearing through the air. A rift opened behind Aris, sucking the heat and oxygen from her lungs. She stumbled, coughing violently, blinded by the pressure shift. Talos stepped forward, grabbed her by the throat, and hurled her across the chamber.

She slammed into the far wall with a sickening crack and slid to the floor, motionless.

Thorne let out a primal roar, fury overriding pain. He charged with his gauntlets blazing, absorbing flame and redirecting it into a wave of kinetic force. His punch landed directly against Talos's helm, staggering the general back a step.

But Talos recovered too quickly. He raised his blade and drove it into the ground. The floor exploded beneath Thorne's feet. Lava gushed up in a geyser of fire, and Thorne was thrown across the chamber like a comet, slamming into the stone in a heap.

Silence hung over the chamber for a heartbeat. The crew was down...broken, bruised, and battered.

Talos stepped toward the Heart, now glowing with intensified fury. Steam hissed from his armor as the power resonated with his corrupted core. "Enough games," he said flatly, as if tired of a child's tantrum.

Aris stirred slightly. She reached for her pistols, fingers trembling, vision blurred. "No..."

She forced herself to stand, leaning on the wall. The others were groaning, trying to rise. Ralik's scanner was shattered. Fen could barely crawl. Thorne was unconscious, smoke rising from his backplate.

But Talos was already moving. He raised his ringed hand, and the air around it shimmered with unseen force. The Heart pulsed violently above the magma, resisting, then slowly, inexorably, it began to descend. Aris screamed and stumbled forward, her last strength pushing her. But she was too late. The heart came to him. Talos raised his ringed hand and plunged it into the Heart's core.

A blinding surge of molten light erupted across the chamber. The shockwave hurled Aris backward like a leaf in a storm, slamming her into the wall again. Her pistols flew from her hands, clattering uselessly across the floor. Her body crumpled.

The second Heart dissolved into Talos's chest, swallowed like a forgotten promise. A rumble shuddered through the chamber as if the volcano itself felt a loss. The earth cracked beneath their feet. The altar split down the middle. Lava burst from the seams, flooding the floor. The entire volcano groaned like a god waking from death.

Talos stood above them, his silhouette distorted by heat, his presence more commanding and powerful than it had ever been.

*Did he also absorb the Velmora Heart?*

"This," he said coldly, "is what power looks like."

Then he turned and vanished, disappearing into the inferno as the mountain roared.

The chamber convulsed around them, the walls splitting and bleeding lava like open veins. Molten rock poured down the altar steps, consuming the platform where the second Heart once hovered. Heat shimmered in every direction, warping air and stone alike.

Thorne dragged himself to his feet first, bruised and scorched but alive. "Aris!" he shouted, spotting her crumpled form near the wall.

She stirred weakly, coughing from the smoke, her voice cracked. "I'm fine...get the others."

Ralik was slumped near a column, cradling his fractured scanner. Fen, bleeding from his temple, clutched his ribcage. Thorne sprinted to them both, crouching beside Fen and hooking an arm under his to support him, while Ralik stumbled upright, leaning hard on the wall.

A tremor ripped through the floor, nearly throwing them all down again. Cracks spiderwebbed toward the entrance tunnel, and molten pressure surged behind them. But before they could run…The fire paused. Not the heat, nor the lava, nor the death tumbling toward them. But time itself…*bent*.

Light gathered above the ruined altar. A pulse. A hum. Then descending through the smoke and fire came the ethereal form of the Guardian.

His shape was blurred, half-light, half-memory. The same celestial presence that had blessed their gear now hovered between them and annihilation, veiled in radiant flame.

His voice was not loud but could be felt throughout the opening. "**You are not ready. But you are chosen.**" They froze, even as the volcano buckled around them. "**He carries two Hearts now. He will seek the last two and when he finds them, the stars will bleed.**"

Aris force herself upright, ash streaked across her face. "Then how do we stop him?"

**"Your journey is not over. It has only begun. Find the other Guardians. Awaken what sleeps. The stars have not abandoned you."** Then he vanished with no blaze, no flourish. Just gone, like a gust of wind. The moment snapped. The volcano surged again, belching molten rock as the chamber caved in around them.

Ralik turned first, eyes wide behind his shattered visor. "The exit, we've got to move!" He quickly grabbed the scattered gear.

"Go!" Thorne shouted, scooping Aris into his arms without hesitation. She didn't resist. Her body went limp, eyes barely open as she clutched her side.

Fen staggered to his feet and ran behind Thorne. Despite the searing pain lancing through his body, he pressed forward, teeth gritted, determined not to let it slow him down. Behind them, chunks of the ceiling crashed down like falling meteors, each strike shaking the ground harder than the last.

They darted toward the escape that twisted downward, steep and narrow, the heat a living thing chasing at their heels. Walls glowed with magma veins, and steam hissed from cracks around their boots.

Ash swirled like a storm around them, thick and choking, turning every breath into a battle. The heat was relentless, pressing in from all sides, baking the tunnel walls until they glowed with veins of orange light. Each step forward felt heavier than the last, like the mountain itself was trying to pull them back into its wrath.

Ralik pushed ahead through the smoke, his hand guiding him. He could barely see, but his memory of the tunnel layout, combined with the flickering feedback from his cracked scanner, gave him enough to lead. "This way!" He called out, his voice rasping against the roar behind them. "Just a little farther!"

Behind him, Thorne was a solid silhouette, cradling Aris in his arms with grim determination. Her armor was scorched, her face streaked with ash, but her chest still rose and fell. Fen, holding his sides but quickly followed. Every few steps he stumbled, the tunnel quaked beneath them, but he kept moving.

Light, real, flickering sunlight finally appeared at the far end of the tunnel. Not molten or hellish, but natural, open-air light. Hope.

The crew surged toward it in a final push, lungs burning and armor scratched raw. They emerged from the tunnel in a staggered rush, collapsing onto a jagged outcropping just outside the collapsing fortress. The air here was still thick with smoke, but it moved, swept by mountain winds rather than suffocating pressure.

Behind them, the volcanic castle was no longer a stronghold. It was a beast in death throes. Fire shot from cracked towers. Lava burst through shattered stone in thick rivers that seared the mountain's flank. The fortress screamed as it died, stone grinding against stone, echoing through the valley like thunder rolling through a canyon.

Thorne dropped to his knees, still clutching Aris, who coughed weakly in his arms. Her eyelids fluttered open, and her gaze slowly focused on the sky. It was a deep blood red, lit by the glow of the volcano and the remnants of a sun choked behind smoke.

She blinked, grimaced, and whispered, "He has two now…"

Her voice was thin, like wind across cracked glass. Thorne nodded, his jaw tightened as he looked back toward the burning mountain. Beside him, Ralik sank to the rock, groaning as he leaned back against the stone, his face pale with pain. Fen crouched beside them, his arm cradling cracked ribs.

For a long moment, they caught their breath. Around them, the groan of collapsing walls echoed through the haze, joined by the hiss of steam and the low, living rumble of a world torn open. They had lost. Not everything, but enough to leave scars.

But as the smoke swirled and the ash fell like black snow, something endured in them still. They had survived. They had escaped. Yet, somewhere in the galaxy, Talos now held two of the Hearts. His power was growing, but so was their resolve. This wasn't the end.

# Chapter 21

## CONFESSION IN THE COSMOS

The ground beneath them still trembled, but the worst of the eruption had passed. The castle was gone, consumed by fire and falling stone, its black walls buried beneath rivers of molten red. In its place, the volcano roared like a god unchained, spewing volcanic ash high into the sky and painting the horizon in shades of ruin.

Aris leaned against Thorne's side, her breaths shallow, chestplate scorched and dented. Her skin was smeared with soot and sweat, blood at her temple beginning to dry.

Ralik sat on a rock nearby, his scanner flickering weakly in his visor. He tapped the side panel and sent out a short-range signal flare, coded with their ID frequencies. If the Zephira Dawn was still intact back where they landed, it would register the ping.

Fen sat cross-legged on a rock, cradling his side. His rifle lay across his knees like a sleeping beast. He squinted into the smoke-clouded sky, looking for the glint of salvation.

It came as a low hum, soft at first, then louder. A pulse of light parted the ash overhead, and through it descended the familiar curved wings of the *Zephira*

*Dawn.* The ship was scorched from the planet, its hull marred with heat streaks, but it flew like it always had.

The landing struts hit the uneven terrain with a groan, and the rear ramp dropped open, flooding the rocks with blue cabin light. Ralik helped Fen up. Thorne didn't let go of Aris as they moved together, limping toward the ramp.

Inside the ship, the lights dimmed automatically, adjusting to the crew's scorched vision. Medkits dropped from ceiling compartments. Oxygen levels normalized. Clean air rushed into their lungs like a forgotten luxury.

"I will never take oxygen for granted again," Fen muttered as he dropped onto the padded bench.

Aris collapsed into one of the reclined chairs, head tilted back, eyes fluttering shut. Thorne stood beside her, unmoving, acting as her shield even now.

Ralik slumped against the bulkhead, tearing off his cracked visor and resting it beside him. For a long moment, the only sound was their breathing and the faint hum of engines adjusting.

The *Zephira Dawn* lifted from the scorched cliffside with a low rumble, her thrusters stirring waves of ash across the blackened earth. Inside the cockpit, Ralik slid into the pilot seat, his fingers moving over the controls with practiced urgency. He winced slightly from his injuries but ignored the pain. More than anything else, they needed altitude, distance, and time to breathe.

"Engines stabilized," he muttered, voice steady despite the exhaustion in his bones. "Trajectory set. Climbing now."

Through the cockpit windows, the volcano shrank beneath them, no less menacing, but distant now. Its lava trails pulsed like veins across the land, and the remnants of the obsidian castle were barely visible beneath the flowing fire.

From the co-pilot's chair, Thorne checked the ship's external sensors. "Residual energy from the eruption's minimal at this height. We're clear of the worst."

Ralik nodded, adjusting the angle of their ascent. "We'll coast past the upper atmosphere until we can regroup with our reinforcements."

The ship breached the last of the smoke veil and entered the upper stratosphere, where stars peeked through the haze and quiet returned to the edges of space. Inside the ship, the flickering red alarms faded to standby blue. The vibration beneath their boots eased.

Aris remained in the medical berth, her armor peeled away in strips to reveal bruised skin and fading burns. Fen administered scans silently, his own body stitched with fresh bandages, his eyes flicking between vitals and atmospheric reports.

"Our ascent is clear," Ralik finally called over the comms. "Focus on healing up."

The words carried more weight than the situation. Rest wasn't just an action, it was a necessity at this point. A release. A quiet acknowledgment that, for tonight, they'd survived.

Aris let out a long breath and slowly sat up, pulling the remaining straps of her armor free. Her gaze drifted toward the cabin corridor where shadows stretched in the low lighting, Thorne had entered, leaning against the wall in silence, and Ralik's voice hummed through the speaker.

They had survived. And for the first time since they stepped foot on Ignarok, the heat wasn't from fire or ash...but from the soothing warmth of still being together.

The hum of the *Zephira Dawn* was as low as a lullaby to the exhausted crew. Fen had long since collapsed into his bunk, snoring softly under a half-pulled blanket, one boot still on. The ship's lights were dimmed in night mode, casting everything in hues of soft amber and deep blue. The worst was behind them, for now.

Aris stepped into the common area barefoot, her hair still damp from a quick rinse in the shower, loose strands falling across her collarbone. She wore one of the ship's sleep shirts, long enough to pass as casual but still clinging to her form in a way that felt vulnerable. She padded across the metal floor with a caution born from unspoken thoughts.

Ralik was already there, half-seated on the edge of the lounge couch, staring out the small viewport. The stars drifted past like sparks in water, silent witnesses to the storm they had just endured. His hands were bandaged, a cup of iced root tea between them.

He glanced back at her and offered a faint smile. "Couldn't sleep either?"

She shook her head and sat across from him. "My mind won't stop racing."

Before either could say more, the door hissed again, and Thorne stepped in. He had changed into dark sleep pants and a loose, half-unzipped jacket, his hair damp, his movements heavier than usual. His eyes flicked between the two of them: Aris leaning forward with her arms wrapped around her knees, Ralik resting against the couch like a man holding back the world, and something in him softened.

"I figured I wasn't the only one up," Thorne muttered. He crossed the room, sat beside Ralik, and dropped his head back against the wall. The pause between them wasn't awkward, it was shared, thick with everything they'd survived and everything they hadn't said.

For a long moment, none of them spoke. Just the low hum of the ship. Just the stars. Then Aris broke it, quietly. "I thought we'd die down there."

Neither man argued. Ralik finally spoke, voice low. "We should have. Talos...he was more than we imagined."

Thorne gave a low grunt of agreement, then glanced at Aris. "But we didn't. Thanks to your leadership."

She met his eyes, something unreadable there. "I didn't save us. You both did."

Ralik's fingers flexed around the mug. "Does it matter who did? We only got out because we were together."

The words settled between them, familiar and steady, like truth worn smoothly by time. Aris showed relief tangled with exhaustion, and something deeper beneath it, something unspoken that had always been there. Her gaze moved from Ralik to Thorne and back again.

"I don't know what comes next," she whispered. "But I'm glad we are together."

Neither of them pulled away when she stood and crossed the small space between them. Neither of them said a word when she sat between them, hands reaching out, not to one, but to both.

Their fingers found her. In that moment, the weight of the mission, the future, all faded, eclipsed by the heat between them. The space between breaths. The closeness of skin and trust and ache.

Aris let herself lean in, drawn not to one heartbeat but two. Her forehead brushed Ralik's first, his breath catching slightly, then turned to Thorne, whose hand slid to the small of her back. There was no hesitation. Just a convergence of their tension, boiling up like the volcanic fire they had just escaped.

Thorne's touch was grounding, strong, calloused, and certain. He held her like he'd been waiting a lifetime, his usual restraint melted away. Ralik was quieter in his affection, slower, but just as steady. His lips found her shoulder gently and he traced kisses down her arm until he met her hand. She touched his cheek, and he kissed her hand.

She belonged to both in that moment, and they to her. Armor had protected them in battle. But here, bare skin against skin, fingers tracing lines of weariness and want, they found a different kind of strength.

Clothes slipped away in pieces, not rushed, but reverent. They kissed like survivors. Like people who had bled and nearly died and now clung to life and light with desperate affection.

Thorne kissed her neck while Ralik's hands moved with reverence across her body. Her breath mixed with theirs, the heat between them building with every exchanged look, every whispered name. The quiet hum of the ship wrapped around them, a shell of safety after chaos.

Ralik guided her down gently, his touch patient, like he wanted to touch every inch of her. Thorne followed, his hands tracing over her curves, his mouth finding places that made her shiver and sigh. Their movements weren't rushed; they were deliberate. Like they knew they might never have this again. Like they intended to make it last.

The couch was too small, so they shifted to the floor, a tangle of limbs and whispers and warmth. Aris laughed once, breathlessly, as Thorne teased her chest with rough fingers, and Ralik met her eyes, lips curling into a soft smile that made her chest ache. That night, she wasn't just a captain, or a fighter, or the one holding everything together. She was wanted. Cherished.

She felt everything. The way Thorne's hands gripped her hips. The way Ralik kissed the inside of her thigh with a tenderness that made her whole body ache. Her breath came in staggered waves, each one chased by the next as they filled her, one after another. One with powerful heft, the other with surprising depth, their devotion overwhelming, their presence impossible to ignore.

She couldn't hold back the flood that built inside her. Her body responded before her mind could catch up, tightening, spiraling, and finally releasing in waves that left her gasping, toes curling, her voice caught somewhere between a moan and a prayer. And when she thought she'd crested the last peak, one of them would pull her back into their rhythm, and the cycle would begin again.

Her fingers clawed against muscle and fabric. Her spine arched. Her vision blurred. Every inch of her burned, not with pain, but with overwhelming, soul-deep pleasure. She was seen. Held. Worshipped.

When the haze finally ebbed and the room fell quietly, Aris collapsed between them, her chest heaving, her heart thundering. Her skin still hummed from the electricity of their touch, every nerve ending aware of where they'd lingered. She felt full, emotionally, physically, completely. And for the first time in longer than she could remember, she felt pure bliss.

They stayed there, arms draped around her like a promise. No words passed. Just warmth. Just breath. Just love.

The next morning the crew stood at the forward deck of the *Zephira Dawn*, gathered beneath the wide observation window where the stars stretched endlessly, unblinking and infinite. The scars of battle still clung to them, scrapes across their armor, bruises along their bodies, burns wrapped in bandages, but they stood tall.

Aris looked at her crew one by one: Fen with his arm in a sling but fire still in his eyes, Ralik focused and calculating even through the haze of fatigue, Thorne silent but steady, a mountain of strength. They were her loyal crew.

"We lost the Heart," Aris said, her voice soft but steady. "Talos has two now. And he'll come for the others. We know that. He's faster. Stronger. But we're not done."

Her eyes met theirs, unwavering. "To stand a chance, we will need the full might of Command. We have to find the next two Guardians and stop Talos before it's too late.

Ralik had already opened a secure channel, patching through the latest reports. Aris stepped in behind him, delivering a clear, concise account of their losses, their findings, and the threat Talos now posed. Command issued orders for a rendezvous with the reinforcements that were approaching. The backup ships would escort the *Zephira Dawn* to the nearest mothership for resupply and further briefing.

Moments later, the crew quietly disbanded, Fen slipping away to the med bay, Ralik muttering something about recalibrating the scanner, Thorne heading toward the weapons locker to inspect the damage.

Joseph Young

Aris lingered behind, fingers brushing the railing near the viewport, her reflection caught in the glass between distant starlight.

Footsteps returned. She didn't look up, but her voice was soft and certain. "I meant it," she said. "Every word. Especially to you."

She turned, just enough for the starlight to catch her cheek, her gaze never revealing who stood there. "I love you."

She smiled, barely a curve of her lips, bittersweet, vulnerable.

And in that moment, the stars kept passing by.

**TO BE CONTINUED**

# Chapter 22

## PIXO S POSTSCRIPT #5

**W**ell...wasn't *that* a volcanic thrill ride?

Our brave crew stormed a molten castle, fought off half the Olyssian army, and stared down a lava-drenched warlord who eats Guardian energy for breakfast. No big deal, right? Just another Tuesday for the *Zephira Dawn*.

And don't even get me started on the romantic fireworks. *Whew!* I might be dead, but I *still* felt the heat coming off those pages. Aris, Thorne, and Ralik let's just say I'll never look at the phrase "ship bonding" the same way again. If anyone's wondering what love looks like in a galaxy burning at both ends...that was it. Tender and steamy enough to fog up a star cruiser's viewport.

Now, as for that ending...I know what you're thinking.

**"Who did Aris confess to?"**
**"What's going to happen with the other Guardian Hearts?"**
**"How can the crew possibly stop General Talos now?"**

Well, welcome to the club, because I'm up here pacing, too.

And you...yes, *you*, the author...I see what you did. Cliffhanger? *Really?* After all that heartache, heat, and heroism, you just drop the curtain like that?

Rude. But also...brilliant.

So, readers, breathe easily (unless you're standing on a volcanic planet), and keep your cosmic compasses tuned. The stars still have stories to tell. And I, your dearly departed feline engineer and eternal fourth-wall breaker, will be watching from beyond.

Until next time.

Keep your plasma charged.
Keep your hearts open.
And for star's sake, pack a towel. You *never* know when a space shower or emotional monsoon will hit.

**—Pixo**
*Rogue Gadgeteer │ Spirit Extraordinaire │ Official Postscript Provider*

# Afterword

Dear Reader,

Thank you.

Whether you tore through these pages in a single night or savored them slowly, I'm truly honored that you chose to spend your time in this universe I created. *Oath to a Withered Star* was a labor of passion, and the fact that you joined me on this journey means more than I can put into words.

As a writer, nothing is more rewarding than knowing someone out there connected with the characters, the adventure, or the emotions woven through the stars. I don't take that lightly, and I promise to keep pushing forward to craft stories that move you, excite you, and maybe even leave you a little breathless now and then.

If you enjoyed this story, I would be incredibly grateful if you left a quick review where you purchased the book, and on Goodreads. Your words make a world of difference...not just to me, but to other readers who might be waiting to take the same leap you made.

You can find information on my other published works, updates, and more on my author page: https://authorjosephyoung.com

Thank you again for being part of this cosmic journey. Until next time. Keep your eyes on the stars.

With gratitude,

**Joseph Young**

# ABOUT THE AUTHOR

**Joseph Young** is a U.S. Air Force veteran, computer science graduate, and lifelong fan of stories that blend action, mystery, and just the right amount of chaos. Born and raised in El Paso, Texas, Joseph has always been drawn to universes where loyalty is tested, the stakes are cosmic, and nothing is ever quite as it seems.

When he's not writing intense space operas or threading plot twists into starlit battles, he spends his time gaming, crafting strategy projects, and exploring new worlds both digital and imagined. He lives with his wife, Sam, and their two amazing kids, Lucille and Lynden, who continue to inspire the heart behind every heroic journey.

*Oath to a Withered Star* is his third published work and marks a bold leap into a high-stakes universe of cosmic power, love, and destiny. The story continues in Book Two...and the stars are watching.

www.ingramcontent.com/pod-product-compliance
Lightning Source LLC
Chambersburg PA
CBHW052029240626
47153CB00006B/2018